"The longer the more trouble I'll make."

Stacie continued defiantly. "I insist you let me go."

"I've no intention of letting you go." Nicholas silenced her protests under the ruthless heat of his kiss, and their bodies melted into each other.

She forgot how much she despised him for making love to her while he intended to marry another. She forgot everything but the magnetism of his body controlling her.

When their mouths parted, Stacie was dazed with passion, terrified by the force of her reaction to Nicholas.

"Don't let me see you with my brother again." His words were like a splash of icy water. Had he been using her body against her? Had that kiss meant nothing to him?

Stacie looked at him coldly. "Your brother and I have something in common. We both hate the sight of you!"

Books by Charlotte Lamb

A VIOLATION
SECRETS

HARLEQUIN PRESENTS

401—SAVAGE SURRENDER
404—NIGHT MUSIC
412—MAN'S WORLD
417—STRANGER IN THE NIGHT
422—COMPULSION
428—SEDUCTION
435—ABDUCTION
442—RETRIBUTION
448—ILLUSION
451—CRESCENDO
460—HEARTBREAKER
466—DANGEROUS
472—DESIRE
478—THE GIRL FROM NOWHERE
528—MIDNIGHT LOVER
545—A WILD AFFAIR
585—BETRAYAL
635—THE SEX WAR
644—HAUNTED
658—A SECRET INTIMACY
668—DARKNESS OF THE HEART
700—INFATUATION
731—SCANDALOUS

HARLEQUIN ROMANCES

2083—FESTIVAL SUMMER
2103—FLORENTINE SPRING
2161—HAWK IN A BLUE SKY
2181—MASTER OF COMUS
2206—DESERT BARBARIAN

These books may be available at your local bookseller.

For a list of all titles currently available,
send your name and address to:

Harlequin Reader Service
P.O. Box 52040, Phoenix, AZ 85072-2040
Canadian address: P.O. Box 2800, Postal Station A,
5170 Yonge St., Willowdale, Ont. M2N 5T5

CHARLOTTE LAMB

scandalous

Harlequin Books

TORONTO • NEW YORK • LONDON
AMSTERDAM • PARIS • SYDNEY • HAMBURG
STOCKHOLM • ATHENS • TOKYO • MILAN

Harlequin Presents first edition October 1984
ISBN 0-373-10731-5

Original hardcover edition published in 1984
by Mills & Boon Limited

Printed in U.S.A.

CHAPTER ONE

'I'M OFF!' Stacie said in William's ear, and he jumped, looking round at her in surprise, his brown hair dishevelled and his tie off.

'I wish you wouldn't creep up on me like that! I get jumpy working in this place with Atkins breathing down my neck.'

Stacie glanced down the long room to where the stolidly ominous figure of the Night Editor was looming over one of the other reporters. 'Giving you a hard time, is he?'

'Is he ever! He's got two of us trying to track down Nicholas Kinsella. I've rung everybody I can think of who might know where the guy is, but nobody is talking. They all say he hasn't left the States, but Atkins got a tip from someone in New York who says Kinsella's over here and up to something.' William massaged his right arm gloomily. 'I'm getting cramp from holding this phone, and I'm beginning to think Atkins is wasting his time.'

'How good is his source, did he say?'

William shrugged. 'He claims the guy is a hundred per cent reliable. I got the feeling it was someone close to Kinsella, but Atkins isn't parting with any names.'

Stacie made a wry face. 'I'm glad I'm getting out of here for a few days. This is a crazy place at the moment, everyone seems to be frenetic. It must be the run-up to Christmas making them so jumpy.'

William shot a wary look down the editorial office, saw that the Night Editor was otherwise engaged, and quickly slid an arm round Stacie's shoulders, pulling her face down towards him. 'Give me a kiss before you go.'

She kissed him lingeringly. The bald man at the next desk watched, saying plaintively: 'Hey, watch my blood pressure! I can't take all this excitement in the office at my age.'

'Shut up, George,' said William, as Stacie straightened again, the overhead lights gleaming on her auburn hair and giving it the brilliance of newly minted gold. His hazel eyes held warmth as he watched her. He was a slim attractive man in his late twenties with a humorous, lively face and an even temperament; he and Stacie had been seeing a good deal of each other for several months. It was a relationship poised on a knife edge which could go either way at any moment. They were not in love—yet she felt that at any moment it might happen, their friendship could become something very different. They liked so many of the same things, they shared a common attitude to life, she couldn't remember dating anyone she liked more. At the same time she instinctively did not want to hurry into love, she wanted their feelings to grow naturally. She did not want to turn on the heat too soon.

'I'd better be on my way,' she said, smiling down at him. 'See you on Monday—and good luck with the Kinsella story. I hope you find him.'

He lowered his voice so that only she could hear him. 'I'd like to get on to his track before Gerry does. We're both in line for the deputy chief reporter job, remember. Atkins will be keeping a close eye on both of us over the next month. I'd like to get ahead of Gerry on this story.' William was ambitious, he was a good reporter and he had a shrewd intelligent mind, but, as in any office, it was necessary to take account of the internal politics of promotion. The Night Editor was an empire-builder, he liked to place his own men, men he could rely on to support him in any office warfare, in key positions and William's chief rival, Gerry King, was one of the Night Editor's drinking buddies and supporters, which meant that William would have to work twice as hard to get the job he wanted.

'What does Atkins think Kinsella is up to over here, anyway?' Stacie asked. It was very warm in the spacious yet crowded room; the central heating was turned right up and all the men were in shirtsleeves and had taken off their ties and undone their collars. Outside the night sky was clear and dark; not a cloud in sight, which meant a heavy frost, no doubt, and icy roads before morning. Stacie had a long drive ahead of her and should be on her way by now, but she was concerned about William. It meant so much to him to get that job.

William shrugged. 'His contact didn't want to say. May not even know. But it has to be something big if Kinsella has come over here himself to sort it out. Nicholas Kinsella doesn't fly the Atlantic just to buy himself a bag of crisps. I wish I had a few of his millions—he wouldn't miss one or two.' He pulled out of the open file on his desk a large glossy black and white photograph. 'Lucky guy! He has it all—money, looks, women. Does it seem fair?'

Stacie looked curiously at the hard-boned dark face in the photograph. Kinsella had been caught in flashlight, his arm around the waist of a beautiful girl in a silver fox fur. Stacie knew the face, although she had never met the man, but then everyone did.

'He's too good-looking for a millionaire,' she decided, laughing. 'I must go, I want to get to Helen's before midnight and the roads are probably tricky . . .'

'Drive carefully, give my love to your sister and the kids and give me a ring on Monday morning.'

Stacie hurried away, blowing him a kiss as she went out of the door. The newspaper was working flat out to get into print by their deadline at ten o'clock. Stacie worked during the day; she was a photographer and was usually on her way home by now, having done a solid day's work from nine in the morning. William was

on the night shift, and didn't leave the office until one
in the morning. It played havoc with their dates; they
had to meet for lunch or on William's free evenings, but
they usually managed to see each other at weekends,
except when Stacie drove down to visit her sister, and
on one occasion William had gone with her because he
had the whole weekend off, a very rare occurrence.
Normally he had to work either on Saturday or
Sunday.

Once Stacie had got out of the busy London area she
found the roads quite empty, but she drove steadily at a
careful speed, because the surface of the tarmac already
had an icy sheen, and she wanted to arrive in one piece.
Stacie had a strong sense of family; she visited her
parents as often as she could, but since they lived in a
remote part of Northumberland she did not see as
much of them as she would have liked. Her sister,
Helen, was five years older and had been married for
eight years to a busy doctor, Roland Laxton, whose
practice covered a scattered rural area in Norfolk.
Stacie managed to see quite a lot of them. They had
three children of whom Stacie was deeply fond.

Helen had never had any interest in a career; she had
married while she was at a teacher training college,
become pregnant within three months and given up any
idea of becoming a teacher. Roland had left the hospital
at which he had been working, got a partnership in a
rural practice and the two of them had settled down to a
quiet, busy life in the country. It obviously suited them,
they were lively, cheerful and contented. Stacie could
not imagine herself leading the sort of life her sister led,
on her visits she was always taken aback by the long
hours and hard work Helen seemed to accept with such
good humour, but then Helen had always had more
energy than was good for those around her, she enjoyed
running other people's lives and was so pleased with her
own that she felt she was in the perfect position to

advise everyone else on how to conduct their affairs. Helen had never, so far as Stacie knew, had a single qualm about her omniscience, but she was so cheerful and warmhearted that most people hesitated to argue with her, they usually ended up doing just as she suggested, which, in turn, reinforced Helen's opinion of her own wisdom.

It was gone ten as Stacie approached the small market town where her sister lived. The streets were deserted, the air frosty and the night still, not a breath of wind stirred the leafless branches of the trees on either side of the road. As she parked on the road outside Helen's house the front door opened and she saw her sister outlined in yellow light. Stacie waved, then walked to the back of the car to get her case out of the boot; she had brought very few clothes with her, but the case was heavy because it was crammed with Christmas presents, most of them for the children.

As she reached the front door Helen said: 'You're late, I was beginning to get worried.' She took the case and gave an exaggerated gasp at the weight of it. 'What on earth have you got in here?'

'Presents,' said Stacie, laughing. 'Happy Christmas.'

Most people were surprised when they were told that she and Helen were sisters; there was no obvious visible resemblance between them. Helen had curly brown hair and brown eyes, she was short and slightly plump and had a round, cheerful face. Stacie was several inches taller, had a slim lithe figure which was perfectly proportioned, thick auburn hair which she wore in a loosely curled style falling to her shoulders, and vivid green eyes which were very expresive. She knew she was not exactly beautiful, but she also knew men looked after her when she walked past. William had told her she had high sex appeal; an animal vitality which attracted the opposite sex. Stacie hadn't been sure she was pleased by the comment. She suspected it meant merely that, like her sister, she had a high energy level. She knew she and Helen had a similar sense of humour and a mutual love for children, animals and the countryside.

'Have a good drive?' asked Helen, placing the case near the foot of the stairs.

Walking stiffly into the firelit sitting-room, Stacie pulled off her gloves and shed her fur-lined suede driving jacket. She was bone-tired and cold, she sank into a chair by the fire and held out her hands to the blaze.

'It was uneventful. There were very few cars on the road.'

'Have you eaten or are you hungry?' Helen picked up her jacket and gloves.

'I'm starving.' Stacie looked round at her with a rueful smile. 'It's nice to be here. I'm looking forward to Christmas with the children.'

Helen smiled back at her. 'I'll get you some sandwiches and coffee.' She went out and Stacie stared at the fire; the room was full of the fragrance of burning pine, a pungent smoky scent which was nostalgic of earlier winters. Woods ran quite close to the back of the house, and Helen had an endless supply of firewood. A little basket of fir cones stood beside the pile of logs on the great stone hearth; in the winter the children enjoyed gathering them for kindling, as they burned a glistening resin oozed from them, scenting the whole room.

By the window stood the Christmas tree; gleaming with coloured fairy lights that flashed on and off at regular intervals, smelling of pine and fresh air, the green branches loaded with glass balls and little home-made decorations which she guessed Helen had helped the children to fashion. Stacie smiled to herself, yawning, her head falling back against the chair. She was incredibly sleepy in the lazy warmth of the room after that long, cold drive.

Helen came back into the room with a tray, cups rattling, and Stacie jolted awake. 'Were you asleep?' asked Helen in surprise, and Stacie yawned, shaking her head.

'Just napping.' She looked greedily at the sandwiches. 'I'm so hungry, these look delicious.' She took one and bit into it while Helen poured the coffee.

'What a pity William couldn't come—maybe next year? By then . . .' She broke off as Stacie gave her a sharp look.

'Don't cross my bridges for me, Helen!'

'I was beginning to think you'd never get married!'

'Who mentioned marriage? William and I have had a few dates, that's all. That doesn't entail a marriage licence, not in this day and age.'

'You brought him to stay with us! You've never done that before. I could tell it was something special.' Helen had always felt free to comment with brutal frankness on Stacie's private life. 'About time, too. You're twenty four, you know'

'That isn't senility, for heaven's sake! I'm in no hurry to get married.' Stacie bit crossly into a sandwich. 'Where's Roland?' she asked, changing the subject.

'Out. He had a call an hour ago. There's been some sort of accident at Emberly Hall.'

Stacie wanted to keep her mind off the subject of William, so she deliberately asked: 'Where's that?'

'A big estate on the Norwich road, you must have seen it as you drove into town—you get a glimpse of the house as you reach the top of the hill. It has a big park round it, you can just see the house through the trees. It's an enormous place, has two farms and a well-stocked lake. The house is eighteenth-century. There was a lot of talk when Mr Kinsella bought the place . . .'

'Did you say Kinsella?' Stacie had sat up, wide awake now.

Helen looked surprised. 'Yes, he's the owner. I've never met him, nobody has—he's never there. I can't think why he bought the place. Some people say he's trying to get planning permission to build on the land. You know what gossips country people are—they're afraid he may build a huge housing estate on the park. Other people say he's going to build an industrial centre, but . . .'

'What's his first name?' Stacie interrupted, and Helen stared at her, brow furrowed.

'I can't remember. Why?'

'Is it Nicholas?'

'Nicholas? It could be, it sounds familiar—why, you don't know him, do you? They say he's a millionaire, an American. Is he famous? He isn't an actor or something, is he?' Helen leaned forward, fascinated and curious.

Stacie laughed, suddenly amused by that idea. 'No, he's a financier.'

Helen looked disappointed. 'Oh. I've never known quite what that was . . .'

'He's the brains and the power behind Kinsella–Moell International. They're a huge international banking concern, they're so rich they lend money to governments and other banks.' Stacie grinned, her green eyes rueful. 'And that's as much as I know myself—and I only know that because William explained him to me. If the Mr Kinsella you have here is the Nicholas Kinsella William is looking for then I'd better get on the phone and tell him.'

'It's an unusual name,' Helen commented. 'Roland will know his first name, I expect. All the staff on the estate are Roland's patients.' She looked thoughtfully at Stacie. 'But you know Roland won't talk about his patients; he's very strict about that. He wouldn't even tell me.'

'How long has Roland been gone? What sort of accident had happened?'

'I've no idea,' Helen said regretfully; she hated to admit there was anything she didn't know. 'More coffee?'

'Thanks,' said Stacie. 'I talked to Mother on the phone this morning; she seems fine. She and Dad are hoping to get down here by Boxing Day, she said, but they want to spend Christmas Day in their own home. Are they staying with you long?'

'A week. They're going to try to get here by tea time on Boxing Day, so you'll have a few hours with them before you start back to London.'

'Good. I brought their presents with me. I got Dad a new pair of binoculars for his bird-watching and I managed to find Mother a Victorian silver thimble for her collection.'

'She'll love that,' said Helen, and began to tell her what she had bought for their parents. Stacie sipped her coffee, eyes half closed, on the edge of sleep but forcing herself to stay awake until Roland returned. Several times she thought she heard a car slowing outside, but it wasn't for half an hour that Helen lifted her head and said: 'There's Roland.'

Stacie listened. 'Are you sure?'

'I'd know his car anywhere.' Helen got up and went out, and a moment later Stacie heard Roland's voice in the hall. He walked into the room, his face ruddy with health and the cold night air, his dark brown hair windblown.

'Hallo, Stacie,' he said, bending to kiss her cheek. His face was chilly from the wind but his eyes were warm. He was in his middle thirties, a forthright, sensible man with a firm manner and a great deal of common sense, his features attractive without being handsome, his blue eyes shrewd and direct, his chin slightly obstinate. He and Helen made a matching pair; their marriage had been a very happy one, they almost never disagreed, and although they might sometimes tease each other it was always with affection and, Stacie knew, a mutual admiration.

'It's good to have you here for Christmas,' he told her.

'It's wonderful to be here,' Stacie said, smiling at him.

'You should have brought your young man with you. Helen's planning the wedding down to the last buttonhole, I hope you realise.' He looked amused as she groaned.

'I wish she wouldn't!'

'You know your sister!'

'All too well!'

Roland sat down in the chair opposite, his body relaxed. 'I'm going to have a cup of hot chocolate and then I'm off to bed—I have surgery tomorrow at nine.'

Stacie studied him uncertainly. 'Roland, the guy who's bought Emberly Hall . . .'

Roland laughed, amusement in his eyes. 'I know, Helen told me—I've no idea if he is the same man and I don't know his christian name. I've never met him, he's never at the Hall and he isn't one of my patients.'

'What was the accident you were called to deal with?' Stacie was disappointed and her face showed it, her green eyes losing some of their excitement.

Roland hesitated. 'I can't see why I shouldn't tell you that—the housekeeper at the Hall had emptied a pan of boiling water over her foot—I've sent her off to the Cottage Hospital for the night. It was a nasty accident, she was in a great deal of pain.'

'Did you see anyone else?'

'Her husband—and he certainly isn't an international financier. He's the head gamekeeper. The owner sends shooting parties down every week in the autumn. Whoever he is, he doesn't use the place himself, it seems to be some sort of conference centre for a big firm.'

Helen came into the room with a cup of hot chocolate and Roland took it, smiling at her. 'And that's all I'm going to say about the people at the Hall. I'm not supposed to gossip about my patients, you

know.' He sipped his drink, his eyes half-closed. 'Mmm
. . . delicious! You shouldn't drink coffee at this hour,
Stacie, it'll keep you awake.'

Stacie watched him, frowning. 'Have you been into
Emberly Hall itself? Is it very grand?'

'I wouldn't know. I went to the back, the servants'
quarters. Getting into the place is like getting into the
Bank of England, though. They have a guard on the
gate and I'd swear he was armed. He made me show
him my driving licence before he'd let me in—and the
gate is controlled from the house, it's electrically
operated. They have some sort of electric fencing along
the walls, too. As I drove up to the house I saw guard
dogs loping across the lawn. I wouldn't like to meet
them if I wasn't safely locked inside a car.'

'That's a lot of security to have around if there's
nobody at home,' Stacie said slowly.

'No doubt the house is full of valuable antiques,'
Roland pointed out, and she nodded.

'I suppose so. All the same, I think I'll ring William
tomorrow morning, he might be able to check it out
from London.'

He gave her a wry look. 'My dear Stacie, even if your
Mr Kinsella does own the house—and even if he's
there, he wouldn't talk to the press, and they wouldn't
be able to get in to see him. I'd say that place was
impregnable.' He got up, ruffling his hair. 'I'm off to
bed—goodnight.'

'I think I'll go too,' Stacie told her sister, reluctantly
forcing herself out of the comfortable chair by the fire.
'Want any help clearing these things away? I'll take the
tray, shall I?'

'No, I'll do that, you get off to bed—you look tired.
Come down for breakfast whenever you like, there's no
need to get up early. Have a good rest.'

Helen was already gathering up cups and plates.
Stacie kissed her lightly and obeyed, so tired that she

fell asleep almost as soon as she got into the warm bed
she found waiting for her. She woke up at nine and by
the time she had had her breakfast it was gone ten
o'clock. She knew William wouldn't be able to talk
much before that hour, anyway; he was a night bird
and found it hard to function properly until lunchtime.
Roland had gone off to his surgery, the children were
playing in the garden, their laughter and shouts drifting
back to the house from time to time. Helen was in the
kitchen making mince-pies, the house full of the smell
of fruit and spice. Stacie rang William's flat and got no
reply, so, rather surprised, she rang the office and was
told by a slightly impatient Day Editor that William
had been sent off late last night to cover a story which
had just broken in Bristol.

Stacie hesitated, frowning. 'I see. Well, when he rings
in will you ask him to ring me as soon as he can? It's
urgent.' She gave the man Helen's phone number and
rang off. She didn't want to give anyone else the news
about Emberly Hall; she wanted William to get the
credit for finding out. He couldn't possibly have known
that Nicholas Kinsella had an estate in Norfolk or he
would have mentioned it, knowing that her sister lived
nearby. Stacie wondered if the purchase of the property
had been discreetly put through without the news
getting out to the press. Perhaps Kinsella had used a
nominee to buy it?

The weather was fine and cold, the sun without heat,
but giving the landscape a gentle gilding which the flat
fields and grey sky needed if they were not to be dull. It
was such a quiet countryside; nothing to see but low-
lying fields on all sides with a few woods to break the
monotony, and here and there the tapering spire of one
of the medieval churches which had been built by wool
merchants during the days when East Anglia was one of
the richest parts of England. That morning Stacie took
the children for a walk to pick up more pine cones for

the fire. Robin was seven, a sturdy, lively boy with his mother's colouring and his father's down-to-earth common sense, and the twins were almost five, two little girls so alike that it was almost impossible to tell one from the other. Stacie could only tell which was Ann and which was Mandy by looking closely; Ann had a small mole on her neck just below her ear. It was the only physical difference Stacie had ever noticed, although in temperament they were quite different! Ann was noisy and high-spirited, Mandy very gentle and reserved.

That afternoon Helen went shopping for last-minute Christmas items. 'I'll take the children with me; they have some presents to get. Are you coming?' she asked, buttoning one of the twins into a pretty pink coat.

'I'd better stay and wait for William to ring,' Stacie said. 'He might want me to check on the house, there must be a way of finding out if it's *the* Nicholas Kinsella who owns it.'

'Can I get you anything while I'm out?' asked Helen, hovering, and Stacie shook her head. She stood in the doorway, waving, as they all drove away, then went back into the house, shivering. She waited for an hour, but William didn't ring. Dusk was settling over the landscape, the air was chilly and a wind had sprung up from the sea, it rattled the windows and wailed through the trees. When the phone began to ring Stacie almost jumped out of her skin. She ran to answer it, and William's voice sounded so near and so familiar that she was breathless for a second.

'What's so urgent? Anything wrong?' he asked.

'William, I think I might have a lead on Kinsella . . .'

'What?' He sounded startled now.

'Kinsella,' she repeated, and told him about Emberly Hall and what Helen had said about the new owner. 'But they don't know his first name; it could be another guy called Kinsella. Maybe you could find out.'

'You're down there,' William said slowly. 'Darling, I'm on a big story here—I can't split off to follow up on this one. Could you see if you can find out if this is Nicholas Kinsella? Get a shot of the house if you can, ask the nearest neighbours, ring the police—you know the form. Someone must know. Try the agent who handled the sale or the police. I'll ring you in the morning, okay?'

Stacie bit her lower lip. 'I'm not a reporter, William, it isn't as easy as you think and . . .'

'Well, do what you can,' said William, his voice impatient. 'Stacie, I must go. I'm rushed for time, there's been a very nasty murder here and the police expect a big break any minute.' He paused. 'Thanks for taking the trouble, I'm grateful, you know that, but . . .'

'That's okay,' she said, and he rang off, promising again to ring her next day. She walked slowly away from the phone, wondering where on earth to start. It was still light enough for her to be able to get a picture of the house, that might be a wise move. It might be slightly grey and blurred, but it would help to identify the place. She never went anywhere without her camera. It had a telephoto lens attachment which she rarely used but which was going to be essential for this occasion. She slipped into her fur-lined jacket, buttoned it up and put on her gloves. She had better hurry before the light went.

Twenty minutes later she was driving along the high stone wall surrounding Emberly House. From the car it was impossible to see anything of the park behind the wall. Stacie slowed as she passed the high, beautifully wrought iron gates, which were shut and obviously locked. Through them she saw a wide drive winding through trees and at the far end of it a white house, only dimly glimpsed and mostly hidden by branches. She wound down her window, stopping the car. Extracting her camera, to which she had already fitted the telephoto lens, she leaned on the door and focused on the house. It was very unsatisfactory to shoot from here, it would give very little idea of the size and appearance of the house, which would be further obscured by the ironwork of the gates, but the pictures would have to do.

She was about to put away her camera and drive on, when she saw a light come on in a downstairs room. A man appeared at a high french window, the light behind him, illuminating his face enough for her to feel a sudden jab of excitement. At this distance it was impossible to be sure, but she was almost certain that it was the man whose picture William had showed her.

Her hands trembling a little, Stacie re-aligned the camera and took some hurried shots of him. He obligingly turned his head and she caught him full face. It was very rare for a picture of Nicholas Kinsella to appear in the media; he was obsessed with keeping both his face and name out of the newspapers, he never allowed the press to interview him and the only time anyone got a picture was when they accidentally spotted him before his security men could spot them and seize their cameras. Stacie couldn't be sure, even now, that she was taking pictures of the man William wanted to find, but it was a chance she couldn't afford to miss.

At this distance, of course, it was a hundred to one shot that the picture would be even vaguely recognisable. The light was so bad and the house so far away and obscured by shifting branches. A sense of burning impatience filled her. If only she could get closer! She looked hurriedly up and down the road. Little traffic used it because it was a side road running parallel to the main road to Norwich, and there was no one about. What she needed was a tree growing close enough to the wall for her to climb up to shoot over the wall. Looking back along the road she saw several trees

which looked promising. She reversed and parked
beside the highest one, got out, slung her camera
around her neck by the black strap which was attached
to it, and considered the tree with a wry expression. It
was a very long time since she last climbed a tree, she
hoped she hadn't forgotten how. It was lucky that she
had put on jeans and a pair of sneakers that morning,
to walk with the children. They would make very
suitable climbing gear. She shed her jacket, slung it into
the front seat of the car, and taking a deep breath
began to hoist herself up. She had been a tomboy in her
childhood, and what she had learned then came back as
she gingerly tested each foothold. It was several minutes
before she reached a branch that splayed out scraping
the top of the wall. Would it take her weight? she
wondered, hesitating. There was only one way to find
out. Cautiously she began to edge her way along it. It
bent but it did not break. Clinging to it, her heart in her
mouth, she finally reached the wall, and stared across
the park.

The light was going fast now; she had to take her
pictures at once. She focused on the house at first, lying
flat along the branch, anchored by one arm, while the
other was free to operate the camera which she
supported on the branch in front of her. The man at the
window had vanished, she saw, to her chagrin, but as
she was about to edge back to safety he appeared again.
He seemed to be staring in her direction, but of course
she realised he couldn't see her. She could only see him
at this distance because she was watching him through a
telephoto lens, an advantage he did not have.

He stood there casually, his hands in the pockets of a
dark suit. Black evening clothes? she thought, taking
some more rapid pictures. He was contemplating the
night sky with an abstracted frown now. Dark-haired,
tall, she guessed he was in his late thirties, and that
hard-featured yet very attractive face was definitely the

one William had showed her in the office. She had
found Nicholas Kinsella! A wave of triumph went
through her. She must get back to Helen's, have the
pictures developed and tell William.

That was when another man appeared. Stacie's eyes
widened in disbelief as they watched him through the
telephoto lens. This second man was someone she
definitely recognised; there was no doubt in her mind
about that! He was an African statesman who had been
in the news recently when he took power in his own
country during a *coup d'état*. It didn't surprise Stacie
that he should be talking to Nicholas Kinsella, but she
had had no idea that Saul Nwanda was in Britain. Was
he trying to get a loan from Kinsella's bank? Was
Kinsella involved in the recent *coup d'état*? She was so
excited and curious that she almost forgot to get a
picture of the two of them together. Realising that
belatedly she hurriedly pulled herself together and
began to take shots of them. Excitement had made her
hands unsteady, the camera slipped suddenly, and she
had to grab at it, her body shifting. That made the
branch bend and she had to cling to it, her arms quickly
grabbing the creaking wood, her legs sliding and
hanging downwards. While she was trying to wriggle
back on to the branch she heard running feet and then a
voice shouting, 'Hey, you! What are you doing up
there?'

Horrified, Stacie shot a look down into the shadowy
park and saw a blur of movement, a man running. At
the same instant she saw the gun in his hands, and froze
in alarm.

She began to slide back along the branch. There was
a sudden stab of orange, then a crack of sound and a
long-drawn-out whine. It wasn't until something
thudded into the trunk of the tree only a few feet from
her head that she realised with dazed incredulity that
someone had shot at her.

'Stay where you are!'

The rough command only made her more determined to get away. She wasn't staying where she was with that gun pointed at her! She had almost reached the trunk of the tree in safety when a line of searchlights was switched on; she hadn't even noticed them hidden along the whole front of the house. They half blinded her, but they also showed her the men running with dark grey wolfish shapes of Alsatians beside them, barking and snarling.

Stacie's mouth was dry with fear. She leapt instinctively, her body tensed, letting herself drop to the ground. It was a long fall, but the only alternative was to be caught still climbing down the tree trunk, and she didn't like the look of those men, their dogs—and particularly their guns.

She landed badly, breathing painfully for a second before she struggled to her feet. A gasp of anguish came from her. She must have sprained her left ankle when she fell. Her car was only a few feet away, though. Gritting her teeth, she began to hobble towards it. It could only have taken a few seconds, but at the time it seemed to be an eternity before she reached the car, her hand fumbling for the door handle.

'Stand still!'

Stacie's pallor increased, but she didn't look round, she pulled the door open without taking any notice of the snarled command. There was another unmistakable crack of sound and a bullet screeched across the top of the car. Her eyes dazedly watched the long scar it left in the white paint; she couldn't believe this was happening to her.

'I said stand still!'

Stacie's head jerked round like the head of a puppet whose string has been abruptly yanked. The gunman halted, mid-stride, a few feet away, his gun pointing at her midriff. Her body seemed to drain of blood, she was ice-cold from head to foot.

CHAPTER TWO

'MOVE!' In case she did not grasp his meaning, the man behind the gun jabbed it sideways towards the open ironwork gates. He wasn't the most prepossessing man she had ever seen; big and broad with a heavy head and scowling brows. Stacie didn't like him, he had no charm, but the gun in his hand made it hard to refuse the implicit invitation. She swallowed and decided to do as she was told.

As she limped towards the gate, biting her lip at the pain that shot through her each time she put any weight on her injured ankle, two men appeared from the shadows, each of them holding the leash of a snarling dog. Stacie stopped in her tracks; she wasn't going anywhere near the bared teeth and snapping jaws, they sent shivers down her spine. The animals barked, pulling on their chains, until their handlers rapped out a command, then both sat, pink tongues lolling out.

'Get a move on!' the man behind her ordered, pushing his gun into her back.

'I've hurt my ankle.'

'Never mind that—walk!'

'I can't!' She lifted her foot, pulled up her jeans and the three men stared at the rapidly swelling ankle. 'It's getting worse,' Stacie said shakily.

The man behind her moved suddenly, taking her by surprise. Before she could stop him he picked her up as though she was a child and slung her over his shoulder in a fireman's lift.

'Hey, what are you doing?' Stacie exclaimed, startled, as he strode towards the gates. She felt stupid hanging down across his shoulder. He smelt of garlic and his

brute strength made her feel helpless and undignified,
he carried her as though she was a sack of potatoes.
Anger streaked through her; when she got to the house
she was going to have a few words to say to Nicholas
Kinsella—how dared he behave like this? It was
perfectly legal to take photographs, this was a free
country, his men had had no excuse for using their
guns. She still couldn't believe they had actually shot at
her. After all, she hadn't even been trespassing. She had
been outside his walls and she hadn't been trying to get
inside them. She hadn't committed a crime.

'Put me down!' she snapped as she saw that they were
at the end of the dark drive, close to the house.

To her fury her captor gave her a light slap on the
bottom. 'Shut up, lady,' he said in what she realised was
meant to be a jocular tone.

She couldn't believe it; her whole body went rigid
with temper. 'How dare you? You hit me! How dare
you lay a hand on me? I'll sue you, I'll complain to the
police—you have no right to hit me, that's a criminal
offence!'

She was still talking in a high, shaky furious voice
when she was suddenly deposited on the ground. She
staggered, her ankle gave way at once, and glared at the
man who had been carrying her. He wasn't looking at
her, though, he was standing very erect and looking
past her towards the open door of the house.

'What's this?' a voice asked; it was deep and brusque
and had a distinct American accent. Stacie heard the
note of authority underlying it and turned her head to
stare, knowing who she would see.

'Caught her up a tree outside, sir, taking sneak
pictures over the wall,' her captor said stiffly.

'Bring her inside.' The other man turned back into
the house, the wind picking up a thick strand of black
hair and winnowing it until he impatiently raked it
down with a firm hand. Stacie saw his face in harsh

profile for a second; the good looks were less in
evidence at that moment, the overriding impression was
of power and force. She felt her stomach sink in dismay.

'You heard what Mr Kinsella said,' the man beside
her muttered, pushing her towards the door. She had no
choice but to obey, her nervous eyes flickering around
the long, high-ceilinged hall into which she was taken.
After the darkness of the park, the menace of the men
with guns, this was a place of elegance and beauty—but
although it should have reassured her, it failed. Her
gaze moved over the golden oak-panelling, the
chinoiserie table on which stood a bowl of white roses
which must have cost the earth at this time of the year,
the delicate porcelain figures displayed on another
table, the vivid colours in the carpet and the shadowy
oil painting dominating one side of the hall, then she
looked at Nicholas Kinsella, her eyes reluctant. He had
walked to the end of the hall and stood in a doorway.

He crooked a long index finger and her captor
pushed her forward. 'All right, Roughton,' Nicholas
Kinsella told him. 'Wait outside.'

Stacie limped with some deliberation, taking her
time, under watchful, appraising grey eyes. The room
was a study, octagonal, richly functional, with books
lining the walls, an enormous stereo unit along one of
them, and in the centre of the room a red-leather-
topped desk covered with neat piles of papers, an office
console unit and several telephones. Behind it was a
deep leather-upholstered chair. She heard the door close,
then Nicholas Kinsella walked past her and sat down
behind the desk while Stacie stood at bay facing him.

He leaned back in his chair, both hands on the edge
of the desk, his fingertips tapping a staccato rhythm
that got under her skin as his narrowed eyes travelled
from her rich auburn hair to the nervous flicker of her
slanting green eyes, down over the warmly curved
mouth that trembled under his stare in spite of her

efforts to hold it steady. When his gaze wandered from her face to an assessing scrutiny of her figure she felt a wave of crimson wash up her throat.

'You have no right to force me to come into your house!' she burst out huskily, infuriated by the way he was staring at her. 'I wasn't on your land. I've a perfect right to climb a tree if I choose! Your men . . .'

'Be quiet!' His voice snapped like a whip and she stopped talking in sheer disbelief for a second before she reacted to the tone, shaking.

'Don't speak to me like that!'

'I'll speak to you how I choose,' he drawled. 'Sit down.'

'No, I won't!' Stacie threw back. She would have refused to do anything he suggested, the words flashed out before she could stop them, but the next second she regretted them because her foot hurt badly and she was dying to sit down.

He surveyed her, his eyes holding irony that made her feel silly. 'I see that you're stupid as well as reckless, Miss . . .?'

'Murray,' she said, then wished she hadn't told him her name. There was no earthly reason why she should tell him anything.

'Have you proof of your identity on you?'

'Of course I have! But why should I show it to you? I wasn't breaking the law, your men were. They shot at me! They deliberately shot at me!' Her face burned with her sense of incredulous outrage, she was stuttering out of rage.

Nicholas Kinsella's black brows drew together, his eyes were hard underneath them. 'Did they hit you?' was all he asked, though. 'I gather they missed,' he went on before she could get around to answering. 'Very careless, if they were aiming at you—they're supposed to be crack shots.' It dawned on her that he was using a mocking drawl, his mouth curling with contempt. 'But then,' he went on drily, 'perhaps they weren't aiming to hit you at all.'

She flushed even more deeply. He had been making fun of her and she didn't think there was anything so very amusing in being shot at, even if the marksman intended to miss. Her dislike of Nicholas Kinsella was rapidly becoming loathing.

'That's beside the point,' she snapped. 'Whether he meant to hit me or not, he shouldn't have aimed in my direction—it was a very dangerous thing to do.'

'Why don't you sit down, Miss Murray, before you fall down?' Nicholas Kinsella murmured, his eyes hooded in weary observation of her trembling figure. 'Are you waiting for me to carry you to the chair?'

Stacie crossly limped forward and sank down with a muffled sigh of relief. Her ankle was throbbing and she could feel that it had become very puffy and hot.

'Why were you taking pictures over my wall, Miss Murray?'

'It's a lovely house, I thought it would make a good picture.'

'You live locally?'

She hesitated, then shook her head.

'Where do you live?'

'That's my business.'

'I think you'll find it is now mine,' Nicholas Kinsella informed her, drumming his fingers on the desk again. She stared at those long powerful fingers, the skin deeply tanned, the nails perfectly shaped and manicured. They had strength, but they also had sensitivity, she could imagine all too easily that they could hurt, but they could probably caress with even more impact.

'You have no right to interrogate me as though I was a criminal! I haven't broken any laws. If you suspect I have, call the police. I wasn't trespassing on your land, I was outside your walls,' she said without lifting her eyes.

'And now you're inside them,' he murmured mockingly, but despite the soft tone she heard the unspoken threat and a little tremor went through her.

'Give me your camera,' he said, stretching out one of those dangerous hands, and she shook her head.

'How old are you?' he asked then, and she looked up, surprised.

'Twenty-four.'

'Old enough to know when it's wise to do as you're told,' he observed. 'Are you a reporter?'

Stacie opened her eyes wide in pretended amazement. 'A reporter? No, of course not! If you won't call the police I'll . . .' She leaned forward to pick up the nearest telephone and he moved abruptly, his hand shooting out to catch her wrist, the gesture sending a ripple of muscled power through the wide shoulders beneath his smooth evening jacket. Stacie winced at the iron grip; his fingers seemed to crush the bones in her wrist. He might be more elegantly dressed than the gunmen he had prowling through his grounds, his clothes expensive and well-made, his thick black hair carefully brushed back from his lean clean-shaven face, a heavy gold watch chain looped across the tight-fitting waistcoat which she could just glimpse under his open jacket, but his power had the same lethal menace.

'Sit down!' The two terse words were bitten out between his teeth, she saw his lip curl back in an angry snarl, and decided it would be wiser to do as he ordered. As she sank back his fingers unclenched from her wrist, and she massaged her reddened skin, frowning.

'If you don't allow me to leave now, the minute I do get away I shall go straight to the police and make such a fuss you'll wish you'd never set eyes on me!'

'I wish that now,' he said drily. Leaning back again, he extended his hand to her. 'Now—your camera, please!'

'It was very expensive, I can't afford to replace it. If anything happens to it I shall hold you responsible.'

'You'll get it back when you leave.'

Stacie was so relieved at the implicit promise that she could go soon that she slowly pulled the camera strap over her head and handed the camera to him, watching with resignation as he opened it, took out the film and exposed it to the light before dropping the camera on the desk and flinging the ruined film into a wastepaper basket.

'Now may I leave?' asked Stacie, half rising.

'First, I want proof of your identity,' Nicholas Kinsella told her, and she hesitated, biting her lower lip.

'I'm not allowing you to leave until I know you aren't someone the police might like to interview,' he said drily, so with a shrug she pulled her wallet out of her hip pocket and showed him the driving licence one side of it contained.

'A London address,' he said without looking up.

'That's right,' she agreed, watching him flicking through the credit cards the wallet held. Suddenly she remembered that among them was her security pass for admission to the newspaper building. Her nerves jumped as Nicholas Kinsella's lean fingers slipped past it, then halted. He slowly withdrew it, placed it on the desk and stared at her, his face very hard.

'So. You aren't a reporter.' He tapped the card. 'You're a liar, Miss Murray.'

'I'm not,' she said huskily. 'I'm a photographer, not a reporter. I wasn't lying.'

'In this case it comes to the same thing,' he said, getting up. She tensed, getting ready for whatever he meant to do to her, but he merely walked over to a cabinet and opened it, got out a decanter of whisky and poured himself a glass, adding soda sparingly. Without looking round he asked: 'Would you like a drink?'

'No, thank you,' she said, staring at his powerful back and shoulders. She wished she knew what he was thinking, what he intended to do with her. What was happening on this estate? The place was an armed

camp; why were all those men with guns running
around the park? What could he have in the house that
required such intensive security to protect it?

He turned, holding two glasses, and walked over to
offer her one. 'It's brandy, you need it,' he said when
she shook her head, and she reluctantly accepted the
balloon-shaped glass. He sat down on the edge of the
desk only inches away from her, nursing his own glass
while he contemplated her face.

'Did your paper send you down here?'

'No,' she said, then wondered if it had been wise to
admit as much. She could read nothing from his hard,
controlled face; not a flicker passed over it to betray
what was in his mind. She wouldn't like to have to play
poker with Nicholas Kinsella; you wouldn't have a
chance of guessing what sort of hand he held. She
increasingly felt that she must watch every syllable she
uttered, he was a dangerous opponent.

'Why are you here? Why were you taking those
pictures?'

'I told you ... sheer curiosity, there was nothing
sinister about it. I didn't even know you were in the
house.' That was true enough, she hadn't been sure of
anything, she had made a lucky guess, that was all.

'Yet you know who I am,' he said softly, and she
hesitated.

'I've seen pictures of you—you're a well-known man.
I'd heard a rumour that you'd bought this estate and I
just thought it might be interesting to take a picture of
it. That isn't against the law, anyone driving past can
see the house through the trees, you can't stop people
seeing it, or taking pictures of it.'

'Have you ever heard of invasion of privacy?' he
asked in tones of contempt, and she flushed again.

His cold grey eyes stayed riveted on her face; she felt
as though her skin was being probed by fine, ice-cold
needles. He was co close that she could see the graining

of his skin, the taut bone structure underneath it, the cheekbones starkly powerful and matched by the formidable jawline. His mouth was beautifully shaped, but there was a hint of cynical sensuality about the lower lip at times which Stacie found disturbing, especially when she noticed the faint cruelty of the hard upper lip.

'What were you doing in this part of the country?' he asked, and to give herself time to think Stacie sipped some of the brandy, feeling the warmth of the spirit spread through her chilled body. It gave her a false courage, she lifted her head to smile defiantly at Nicholas Kinsella.

'Visiting friends.'

'Who?'

'I've answered enough questions,' Stacie said firmly, putting down her glass on the desk. 'I'd like to leave now, it's getting late and my friends will start to worry about me. They might ring the police, and you wouldn't want to have to explain to them why you were holding me against my will, would you?' She stood up, and found him on his feet too. He was over six foot, her head just topped his shoulder, and his long body looked as if it was all muscle. Although she was on tenterhooks to get away, at the same time she was aware of his fascination; she had never met a man like him before. He was alarming, even frightening—and yet she knew he was the most attractive man she had ever set eyes on, or was the essential element of his sex appeal that aura of danger he carried around with him?

Stacie had never thought of herself as being the sort of girl who found it exciting to take risks or flirt with danger, but as she stared into Nicholas Kinsella's watchful eyes she felt a prickle of undeniable sexual response. Her breath caught and she looked away.

His hand suddenly took hold of her chin and forced her head up again. Her nervous eyes met his, shifting warily under his stare. 'You've placed me in a dilemma, Miss Murray,' he said softly. 'I'm not sure what to do with you and you aren't being very frank with me. I don't see how I can let you go, I'm afraid I'm going to have to ask you to stay here tonight.'

Her throat beat with a frantic pulse, then she swallowed. 'You can't be serious—that's ridiculous, you can't keep me here against my will!'

'You needn't be alarmed,' he said with a wry twist of that hard mouth. 'You'll be quite safe, I give you my word.'

'You don't honestly expect me to accept your word of honour, do you?' she flared angrily.

'You have no choice in the matter,' he said with a harsh amusement, and she stared back at him, realising how right he was—she had no choice because there was a man with a gun on the other side of that door and she already knew that he was prepared to use it. Shock and fear made her lose her head, she began to stammer furiously, pulling herself free, sinking back into her chair.

'Why can't I leave? What are you up to here? Why are you so afraid of anyone finding out anything about you? Why is Saul Nwanda here?' The name slipped out before she had considered the possible consequences of admitting that she knew that the Prime Minister of Kerosi was in the house, and as she said it she saw Nicholas Kinsella's face tighten, his grey eyes flash and harden. She had made a serious mistake and she could have kicked herself; she shouldn't have let her temper get the better of her. Stacie had always had trouble with her hot temper, it flared up and exploded before she could control it, and a hundred times in the past she had determined never to lose her temper again, only to have it break out once more just when she wasn't expecting it. Her intelligence knew the dangers and Stacie was a girl with a good brain, but although she had managed to hold her temper down until now she had just thrown away any advantage she had gained.

'So, you saw him,' Nicholas Kinsella said slowly. He glanced across the desk at her camera. She was able to follow his train of thought without difficulty; he was wondering if she had taken pictures of Saul Nwanda. 'Or did you know he was here?' His head swung so fast that she found herself looking into his eyes before she had time to think,

'No, I hadn't any idea at all,' she said.

'So you say.'

'It's the truth!'

He kept his eyes on her. 'I hope it is, but in any case it's unfortunate that you saw Mr Nwanda, it means I'll have to keep you here until he's back in his own country.'

Stacie looked down at her foot, fighting down the tremors of anxiety that were making her feel cold and on the point of tears. 'My foot hurts badly. I must see a doctor—I think I've broken a bone.'

He frowned, then knelt down beside her and rolled up the leg of her jeans before he gently untied her sneaker and began to ease it off the injured foot. Stacie flinched, closing her eyes, sweat springing out on her upper lip and forehead. As the pressure of the shoe was removed the throbbing grew worse, she was afraid she would faint.

Nicholas Kinsella's cool fingers felt the puffy swelling. As the worst of the pain subsided Stacie looked down, grimacing.

'It isn't a pretty sight, is it?'

He looked up at her, his grey eyes faintly smiling. 'It isn't broken, either. You've sprained your ankle; so we'll bandage it firmly for you and you can stay in bed for a day or two. Rest is all that's needed.'

For a moment she felt a wave of relief, then she remembered that somehow she had to get away from here. She had to persuade him to send for a doctor, which meant he would ring Roland, and once he had realised that her brother-in-law knew she was here he would have to let her go.

'Are you a qualified doctor?' she asked sarcastically. 'My ankle should be X-rayed, it's the only way to be sure I haven't broken anything.'

Nicholas Kinsella stood up. 'I know a good deal about broken bones. I have a ranch in Arizona, and someone is always taking a tumble and breaking an arm or a leg. It's a long drive to the nearest doctor; I soon learnt to distinguish between a broken bone and a sprain.' He gave her a dry smile. 'Good try, Miss Murray, but you're staying right here.'

She trembled with rage this time, her green eyes flashing. 'You can't keep me here against my will— that's kidnapping! Does it make you feel tough to have men with guns to back you up? I notice you told your hired assassin to stay outside in case you need him. What sort of man are you, anyway? I only have one good foot, you don't need to be scared of me.'

He laughed, watching her, leaning against his desk with folded arms. 'Finished?'

'No, I haven't,' snapped Stacie. 'You can go to prison for a long time in this country for what you're doing—and when I get out of here I'll kick up hell, believe me.'

'I do,' he said. 'You're not doing a bad job of it now.'

'How long do you think you can keep me locked up here? If I don't turn up tonight my friends will ring the police, and they'll start looking for me.'

'Give me their phone number and I'll see that they're reassured about your safety,' he simply said with cool insolence, and Stacie seethed impotently as she stared at him.

With a sudden childish self-pity she said sulkily: 'My foot hurts like hell.'

'I'll put a cold compress on it in a minute and bandage it for you.' He smiled at her wryly, but she wasn't going to be soothed by the brief glimpse of charm she saw in his face.

'You can keep your hands to yourself—I don't want you touching me!'

His brows arched. 'Just as you like, but my housekeeper isn't here at the moment and there are no other women here—would you prefer Roughton to do it?'

'No I wouldn't,' said Stacie, shuddering deliberately. 'I want to see a qualified doctor.'

He sighed, leaning back to consider her. 'Miss Murray, I have very good reasons for making sure you don't leave here for the next day or so. Mr Nwanda is in this country secretly for talks with me—we chose Britain as a meeting place because it was a neutral base we both felt we could trust and I had this house available where we could maintain the very strictest security. It's essential that no news of our meeting leaks out before we're ready to announce it ourselves. It's a great pity that you happened along at this moment, but you can hardly claim you were invited—you arrived, and you must take the consequences. This is a comfortable house, if you're sensible you can enjoy a brief stay here and no harm will be done. If you give me your word you won't try to escape, I'll treat you as a welcome guest.' He looked at his watch with a slightly impatient sigh. 'What do you say?' he went on, glancing back at her. 'Please, don't waste any more of my time. Mr Nwanda is waiting for me, we're about to have dinner. I'm afraid I can't ask you to join us, we're still talking about very private matters, but Mr Nwanda is leaving later tonight to get a plane. Once he's back in his own country I'll release you.'

Stacie looked down, her face uncertain. Reluctantly she saw the common sense in his argument; it sounded very reasonable, and once she was released she could get in touch with William and tell him the whole story. It would make quite a scoop for him, he was certain to get the promotion he wanted.

'Well? Is it a bargain?' Nicholas Kinsella asked, and she shrugged.

'I suppose so. I'm staying with my brother-in-law, Dr Roland Laxton . . .'

'Laxton? He was here yesterday to see my house-keeper,' he interrupted, and Stacie nodded. 'I see,' Nicholas Kinsella said slowly. 'So it was him who told you . . .'

'No, I'd already heard, it's common knowledge around here that a man called Kinsella bought this house. I didn't know for certain that it was you, and Roland is far too discreet to tell me anything about his patients.'

'I'm not one of them,' Nicholas Kinsella told her. 'I've never met your brother-in-law, but everyone who comes through the gates is logged in and out as a routine matter. I knew he'd been here.' He went round his desk and pressed a button. The door opened and Roughton stared at them. 'Will you fetch some lukewarm water and a towel and some bandages for Miss Murray's foot?' Nicholas Kinsella asked him, and Roughton nodded and went out, closing the door again.

'Are you in Norfolk for Christmas?' Nicholas Kinsella asked Stacie. and she nodded, giving a faint sigh.

'I hope you're going to let me leave by Christmas Eve,' she said, half accusingly. 'I always spend Christmas with my sister and her family. Christmas is a time to be with children.' She looked at him curiously. 'Are you married?'

His mouth twisted. 'No; that much you can find out from the reference books—but please don't try to interview me, Miss Murray, because I never give press interviews.'

'I know, that's why the media are so interested in you.' Her dry tone made him smile briefly.

'Sorry to have deprived you of a scoop. Those pictures would have sold well, I suppose.' He didn't sound in the least apologetic and Stacie stared at him with irritated eyes.

'You know very well they would,' she said bitterly, just as the door opened and Roughton came back with a large tray on which stood a bowl of water, a fluffy white towel and a large white metal box with a red cross on the lid. He put the tray on the desk, Nicholas Kinsella stood up and nodded to him.

'Okay, Roughton, I'll bandage the foot. Miss Murray is staying for a while. She can have the pink bedroom, see it's ready for her, will you? She'll eat up there this evening. She has to rest this foot.'

'Yes, sir.' Roughton went out, his face wooden. Stacie watched Nicholas come round towards her, he lowered the tray to the carpet and knelt down.

'Let's have that foot in the water.'

Stacie slid it into the bowl; the lukewarm water lapped gently around her swollen flesh and she sighed with pleasure.

'Feel better?'

She looked down at Nicholas, who smiled at her. 'Yes, thanks.'

After a moment her foot was dried; Nicholas lifted it carefully on to his knees across which he had spread the towel, and delicately patted the wet skin before he bandaged the ankle firmly. He stood up, put the tray back on to the desk and considered her, his head tilted to one side.

'Do you want to be carried again, or will you lean on Roughton and hop? I have to join Mr Nwanda, he must be wondering what on earth is going on.'

'I'll hop,' Stacie said, and grinned suddenly.

'I thought you'd prefer that option. Roughton will
find you a pair of my pyjamas; I don't think my
housekeeper's nightwear would fit you, she's only just
five foot.'

Stacie hesitated. 'Can't you let me ring my sister to
set her mind at rest? She'll be so worried!' He was
behaving more like an approachable human being, she
put all her energies behind the pleading smile and the
gaze of her slanting green eyes, and Nicholas Kinsella
viewed her wryly, his hard face shrewd.

'Don't worry, they'll know within the hour that
you're okay, but I can't let you talk to anyone outside
this house. I've explained why, it's essential that no
word gets out about this meeting.'

'I wouldn't say anything about Mr Nwanda!' Stacie
begged, still optimistic.

'I'm sorry,' he said, and called Roughton, who put an
arm around Stacie's waist and helped her to hop
towards the door. As she left the room she threw a
furious look back towards Nicholas Kinsella, hating
him, but he wasn't looking in her direction; he had
forgotten her already, he was seated behind his leather-
topped desk, opening a large black file and studying it
with intent concentration, the lamplight gleaming on his
sleek black hair and the tanned olive skin stretched
flawlessly over the beautifully sculptured bones.

'Here you are, miss,' said Roughton, throwing open a
door. He helped Stacie to hop to the bed, she sank
down on it, looking around her curiously at the pretty
cream and pink room. It was comfortable and spacious,
the walls covered with a cream paper with a silky
texture which seemed to ripple in the light, the carpet a
very pale pink and the bed covered with a heavy satin in
a deeper shade of pink, a pleated valance hanging to the
floor.

'I hope you'll be comfortable here,' Roughton said.

'There's the bathroom adjoining.' He pointed. 'And I've put some pyjamas on the bed. Dinner should be ready in half an hour. If you need anything dial six on the telephone.' He caught her quick glance and grinned. 'It's an internal phone, miss; you can't make an outside call on it.'

'How useful,' Stacie said sarcastically, and he laughed.

'I took the external phone out, miss. Sorry, I'll have to lock you in . . .' He went out, closing the door and she heard a key turn. There was a bolt on the door, she noticed, so she hopped slowly over and shot it into place with a reassuring click, then explored the bathroom. It held a shower unit with a glass cabinet around it, a small vanity unit and a bath and lavatory and bidet; no expense had been spared to make it a beautiful room. If she had to stay locked up anywhere this would certainly make a comfortable prison, but Stacie seethed with resentment at the idea of being kept in captivity, however luxurious. Being practical, however, she stripped and washed before getting into the pyjamas on the bed, they were far too long for her and as they were made of pure black silk they refused to stay rolled at the ankles, so in the end she impatiently decided only to wear the top. It came down to her thighs, and while she was in the bed nobody would realise she was naked from the thigh downwards. Before getting into the bed she unbolted the door. She was feeling distinctly hungry and she wanted the dinner Roughton had promised to bring her.

It was ten minutes later that she heard a tap on the door, then the key turned and Stacie found herself looking, not at Roughton, but at Nicholas Kinsella. He was carrying a tray, and in spite of her hunger Stacie couldn't think about the food he was bringing her, she was flushing helplessly under the interested, assessing stare of his grey eyes, as they wandered from her recently washed face, innocent of make-up now, to the open lapels of the black silk pyjamas, her smooth bare skin visible between them. Stacie was so aware that he was looking at the soft curve of her breasts that she pulled the sheet up to her throat, her hands unsteady.

'Settled in?' he asked coolly, coming over to put the tray across her knees. 'I hope you like chicken—with my housekeeper out of action we're having to rely on a girl from the village, and this was the best she could do, roast chicken.'

'I thought you said there were no women in the house?'

'You're too sharp, Miss Murray,' he said. 'I didn't want her to see you; she never comes out of the kitchen while she's here, she has no idea who I am and she hasn't set eyes on Mr Nwanda. I want to keep it like that.'

'And you called me a liar,' Stacie murmured with biting irony.

'I've brought you a glass of champagne,' he said, ignoring that. 'Drink it before it goes flat.'

'A whole glass just for me? Gracious, how generous,' said Stacie, picking the glass up and draining it while he watched her. When it was empty she handed it to him with a sweet smile.

Softly he said: 'My pyjamas never looked that good on me.'

She stiffened, looking down.

'They must be rather long for you,' he added probingly, watching the flushed curve of her cheek.

Stacie didn't want him to realise she wasn't wearing the bottom half of the pyjamas. She said tartly: 'Did you ring my family?'

'Yes, that's all dealt with.'

'Oh, is it? And what did you tell them? Not the truth, of course.'

'Naturally not,' he said, moving to the door. 'Enough

to stop them worrying about you, that's all. Enjoy your meal. Some coffee will be along shortly.'

'Must you lock that door?' she demanded as he was about to leave. 'I'm getting acute claustrophobia.'

'Will you give me your word of honour not to try to escape?' he asked, turning to look at her.

She hesitated, then said grudgingly: 'Yes.'

He smiled. 'Then I'll leave it unlocked.' He spoilt this generosity by adding coolly: 'Roughton wil be on guard at the foot of the stairs, by the way, and there's no other way out of the house.'

Stacie threw one of her pillows at him and heard him chuckle as he closed the door. The pillow fell harmlessly to the floor without hitting him. What had he told Roland? What sort of lie had he cooked up? William would ring her tomorrow, he was going to be surprised to find her missing; she wished she knew what Nicholas Kinsella had told Roland—how could he have accounted for her abrupt disappearance? She looked down at the beautifully served balls of pale greeny-yellow melon in a silver dish. They looked good; she put one absently into her mouth and the fruit melted lusciously on her tongue as she thought about William. She couldn't wait to give him this story; it would make front page news. William's career would get a great boost from this. She finished the melon and began to eat the chicken which had been kept hot under a silver cover, wishing she hadn't been so reckless in drinking that glass of champagne too fast, she could do with another glass right now. When she had eaten as much as she wanted she put the tray down on the floor and lay back, feeling lonely. She was sick of these four walls already, she wanted to get back to Helen's and be with them all as they got ready for Christmas. This was her favourite time of year, and now it had been spoilt by Nicholas Kinsella. She wished she had never set eyes on him.

CHAPTER THREE

ROUGHTON brought her some coffee ten minutes later, his eyes politely averted as she hid under the bedclothes. He took her tray and replaced it with another bearing a coffee pot, a silver jug of cream and a sugar bowl, a cup and saucer and a small silver vase with a white rosebud in it. Stacie's eyes fixed on the flower. Had he placed it there? Or had Nicholas Kinsella? She decided not to ask him, he might repeat what she said to his employer.

'Anything you need, miss?' he asked, eyes down.

'No, but don't lock that door. Mr Kinsella said . . .'

'I know, miss, he told me.' Roughton walked heavily out of the room, closing the door behind him, and Stacie hobbled over to bolt it. She heard Roughton's footsteps halt, but he didn't come back, after a second he walked on again. Of course, they knew she couldn't escape out of the window. Even if she did manage to climb down there were those horrible dogs prowling through the park, not to mention Roughton's friends with guns.

She didn't expect to sleep that night. She took her time drinking the coffee, her mind going over all that had happened earlier. In an odd sort of way she was almost beginning to enjoy herself now that she was practically certain that she was in no real danger. It would make a good story for William, she mustn't forget any detail of it.

When she had finished her coffee she lay down, her arms behind her head, wishing she had a book to read. There was a small gold clock on the bedside table, she stared at it as it ticked in a quick, breathless way as though it was running a race with time. The sound was hypnotic and soporific, her eyelids felt heavy, she couldn't keep them open, even though she had deliberately left the light on.

Some time later she woke with a start and for a few seconds couldn't orientate herself. Her eyes flashed around the room, filled with amazement as she realised she wasn't in her own flat, then she remembered where she was and at the same instant realised that she had been woken up by voices; there were people downstairs talking loudly to each other. Stacie slid out of the bed and limped to the chair on which she had neatly folded her jeans. She stepped into them, zipped them up and quietly opened the door, listening.

'Have a good journey, Saul—safe landing!' That was Nicholas Kinsella's voice, raised as though he was calling to someone.

Stacie quietly crept along the corridor to the landing at the top of the stairs. She cautiously leaned on the polished mahogany balustrade and stared down into the hall; there was no sign of Roughton, the front door was wide open and she could see Nicholas's long, dark-clad back as he stood on the threshold, an arm raised in farewell. The winter wind blew past him, ruffling his hair, making the carpets rise and fall and a door bang somewhere. Stacie saw Nicholas turn to come back into the house and hurriedly drew back, her nerves prickling while she listened for a sound which might warn her what he was doing.

A stair creaked and she stiffened. He was coming up here! She backed, her eyes dilated, and bumped into a grandfather clock standing against the wall behind her. There was a little crash, the pendulum clanged protestingly against the walnut casing, the clock twittered like a frightened bird, and Nicholas Kinsella took the stairs three at a time.

'What do you think *you're* doing?' he asked, halting as he caught sight of her, an impatient frown pulling his brows together. He was fully dressed and obviously hadn't been to bed yet, although he had undone his tie which hung loosely around his throat, the black silk slightly crumpled now.

'Mr Nwanda has gone now, so are you going to let me leave?' asked Stacie, her thumbs in the waistband of her jeans. She was trying to look cool and self-confident enough to impress him, if he thought she was nervous he would ignore her.

'Were you eavesdropping?' he demanded, staring at her with hostility. 'I should have locked you in! I might have known you wouldn't stay put. I'm willing to bet that the only thing you know about claustrophobia is how to spell it.' The lines of his face held weariness, though; she watched him and could see that his hours of negotiation with the African statesman had drained him of energy, his skin was pale and his body was held slackly, as though he was standing upright only with an effort.

'How did the talks go?' asked Stacie, and got a sardonic look.

'You don't expect me to answer that?'

'How many million are you lending him?'

'Just how much did you overhear?' he asked, looking very angry. He stared at her and she could see that he was thinking back over his conversation with Saul Nwanda in the hall and wondering how much of it she had heard. Stacie wasn't going to admit she hadn't heard any of it; let him worry, it served him right. She wished she had heard far more; if she had woken up a few minutes earlier she might have picked up some interesting quotes for William, although it was doubtful if the paper would have used them in case of offending Saul Nwanda, she decided, so it didn't really matter.

Something in the grey eyes made her decide to quit while she was ahead, she turned and limped back towards her room, knowing that Nicholas Kinsella was on her heels. Over her shoulder she said lightly: 'You may think you're above the law, but you'll soon find you're not. So far I've counted a grand total of four charges against you: kidnapping, attempted murder, sexual assault . . .'

'What?' His voice rose sharply. Stacie hurried into her room and began to shut the door in his face, her hand fumbling for the bolt, but he leant his whole weight against the other side of it and slowly, inexorably, forced it open again. Giving up the unequal struggle, Stacie fled, keeping an elegant little rosewood table between them.

Nicholas halted, staring at her. 'You've gone too far, Miss Murray,' he said very softly, but the almost gentle tone did not hide the anger in those grey eyes. 'I no longer find you amusing.'

Stacie had flushed, her own anger rising. 'I wasn't being funny!'

'Are you seriously going to accuse me of . . .' His voice broke off and his face hardened even further, his eyes as sharp as steel points. 'Or are you telling me that someone else . . . Roughton? Did Roughton touch you?'

'Touch me? He carried me over his shoulder, slapped my behind when I protested, manhandled me—*you* may think women enjoy that sort of treatment, but I can tell you they don't. I'm not letting either him or you get away with it!'

He had listened, frowning. Now he said curtly: 'You said sexual assault.'

'Would he have slapped a man's behind?' Stacie threw back. 'Or laughed when he did it? If that isn't a sexual assault, what is?'

'It's hardly a very serious . . .' he began, and she interrupted, her eyes flashing.

'I think it's very serious—I objected violently!'

Nicholas ran a hand over his face slowly, wearily, as though trying to expunge the lines of exhaustion from it, and Stacie watched him with reluctant compunction. He looked dead-beat, but she wanted to get away from here and give her story to William before the official news broke. She had to hassle Nicholas Kinsella if she was going to force him to release her.

'Have you any idea what an inconvenience you are, Miss Murray?' he asked after a brief silence, letting his hand fall. 'The last thing I need is a long wrangle with you. I'm tired, I want to get to sleep. Frankly, you've been nothing but trouble, and I'm getting sick of you.'

'Sorry,' Stacie said unrepentantly, and he stared at her with barely restrained irritation.

'Get those jeans off,' he said abruptly, and she stiffened.

'What did you say?'

'I'm taking your clothes with me,' he said, his voice metallic. 'I want to be certain you won't roam around the house for what's left of the night, prying into my affairs. So get your jeans off—or do you want me to take them off for you?'

'Turn your back!'

'On you? You must be joking,' he said drily. 'You'd probably stick a knife into me.'

'Look, I'm not going to . . .' Stacie's angry words choked in her throat as he took a long stride, his hand reaching for the zip. 'Get your hands off me!' She tried to step backwards, but the zip was already sliding down.

She was unaccountably frozen with shock, it was unusual for her to be taken by surprise by a man, but her wits had briefly deserted her. And then Nicholas Kinsella took hold of her hips and pulled her jeans down, and panic surged into her, the adrenalin it brought making her kick out, slapping his hands away.

'Leave me alone!' She kicked the jeans off and limped towards the bed, angrily aware of his eyes fastened on her bare, smooth thighs.

'I thought you had the pyjama trousers underneath your jeans,' he said with a note of apology.

'I bet!'

'Stacie, I did. I wouldn't have . . .' He stopped talking as she turned a flushed, furious face towards him.

'Wouldn't you? Tell that to the police—Saul Nwanda may have diplomatic immunity, but I bet you don't, you're going to have to answer for the way you've been manhandling me! And don't think you'll be able to buy your way out of it, because I'll make sure you don't!'

He didn't answer. He was staring down into her face, but she didn't get the feeling he was listening to her, there was a strange look in his eyes, his black pupils enlarged and glittering as though he was drugged. Stacie stopped talking, a silence fell, they stared at each other as if they had just met for the first time and she was suddenly breathless; her whole body burnt with unexpected heat and her lungs snatched audibly at air as Nicholas Kinsella slowly lowered his gaze to her parted mouth.

Stacie tried to say something, break the strange spell holding her, but she couldn't make her lips move, her tongue had frozen in her mouth. She knew he was going to kiss her. She should do something to stop him, but she waited for it with hypnotised passivity.

He lowered his head so slowly that her nerves screamed, her mouth was dry with anticipation as his mouth closed over hers. She was intensely conscious of that first touch, their flesh meeting warmly, merging, with a fast-building heat that rapidly got out of her control. He put his arms round her, pulling her closer; Stacie's arm went round his neck and her fingers clutched at his hair, tightening on the thick, smooth strands as his kiss took on a new hunger, a demand she met without attempting to pull away.

When he raised his head again she had her eyes

closed and was reluctant to open them. Her pulses were hammering with a rhythm she had never felt before, she didn't want him to stop kissing her, she felt cold and bereft as his lips left hers.

Nicholas was staring down at her, exploring the shadowy cleft where her warm flesh flowed against the black silk, the pale curve of her round breasts just visible, then watching the way the top clung damply, moist with perspiration now, to her waist and hips, showing every curve of her body as clearly as if she was naked. Stacie saw the glitter in his eyes and went into panic, trembling violently, as though she was facing a dangerous animal.

She shuddered at the image—there is no animal more dangerous than man, and she had never been so conscious of being a female confronting a male, one so much stronger than herself that his masculinity was a threat even when he wasn't overtly threatening her.

She forced herself to say something, her voice shaky. 'That's enough!'

'Not for me,' he said huskily, kissing her throat with a deliberate sensuality that undermined her attempt to refuse to go on; the languorous slide of his lips on her skin wringing moans of pleasure out of her. She twisted in his arms, her hands on his shoulders, then his mouth came down fiercely against her lips and her brief struggle was over, she swayed closer to kiss him back.

He undid the buttons of the top; one hand sliding over her bare midriff before it moved up to caress her breasts; his other hand followed the line of her spine, his fingers softly brushing the tiny hairs marking the indentation in her flesh, and each touch intensified her hunger for the pleasure he was giving her, she breathed so fast it hurt, kissing him passionately. His knee pressed between her legs, his warm fingers splayed across her buttocks, the weight of his body urging her backward to where the bed stood waiting for them.

'Mr Kinsella! Mr Kinsella, where are you?'

The voice broke into their hectic excitement and Nicholas lifted his head, his grey eyes brilliant with aroused desire, his face taut. Stacie heard heavy footsteps on the stairs and Nicholas let go of her, his flush deepening.

'What the hell now?'

'Mr Kinsella . . .' The voice was much nearer and Stacie recognised it.

'It's Roughton,' she whispered, dazed and in shock, and Nicholas swore under his breath.

'Damn him!'

He left so suddenly that the door slammed after him, making her jump, and she was so strung-up after their lovemaking that tears came into her eyes and she sat down on the bed, shaking from head to foot, her teeth chattering and her body icy cold as the heated desire drained out of her. She wrapped her arms around herself, rocking to and fro like a frightened child.

How could she have let him make love to her like that? She hated herself; how could she have behaved in that way? It didn't mean anything, it couldn't mean anything, he was a million light years out of her class and they barely knew each other. What on earth could he think of her? But she knew that, it was obvious, he thought she was an easy lay, and she couldn't blame him after the way she had just let him make love to her. She had made a token protest and he had pushed it aside, smiling; he had known she didn't mean it, he must despise her, and when he had settled whatever Roughton had to say to him he would be back, expecting to pick up where he had left off, convinced that she would be waiting for him in this bed. It wasn't going to be easy to persuade him that she wasn't going to sleep with him tonight.

Stacie couldn't remember ever losing her head like that before; she had never been promiscuous, her self-respect wouldn't allow it. She was appalled as she remembered how fast he had gone; within five minutes of first kissing her he had been pushing her towards the bed, and she hadn't been struggling. Even now she felt a deep ache of frustration in the pit of her stomach; she had wanted him.

She put her hands over her face, sick with self-disgust. She must be crazy! What was the matter with her? What was she going to do when he came back? The very idea of it electrified her into action, and she got off the bed and hobbled towards the door to bolt it, then with her hand on the panels froze, listening, at the sound of the voices below.

That was a woman's voice! Stacie pulled the door open to make sure she wasn't imagining things, and limped rapidly along the corridor to lean on the balustrade and look down into the hall.

It was empty. There was no sign of Nicholas or Roughton, but the lights were blazing and a pile of luggage stood by the front door: expensive suitcases, cream pigskin with initials stamped in gold on the locks. Whoever had arrived did not travel light.

Stacie wanted to look more closely, find out whose initials those were; she crept downstairs, alert to any sound, but just as she reached the hall Nicholas strode from the other end of it and halted, seeing her, his face harsh.

'Get back upstairs!' he snapped with such ferocity that Stacie began to obey him without argument, her nerves shot to pieces by now.

She had only taken one step, however, when a door opened at the far end of the hall and she heard quick, light tapping footsteps. Stacie swung round, startled, as a clear, peremptory voice demanded: 'Nicholas, whatever are you doing? You've been . . .'

The voice trailed off into stunned silence as the newcomer saw Stacie, who was frozen into immobility at the sight of her.

'Good heavens . . .' the woman breathed. She was middle-aged, with stylish silvery hair curling around a carefully made-up face, her pale blue eyes set well apart, beautifully spaced, under finely defined brows which had risen almost to her hairline as she slowly inspected Stacie from head to foot. She didn't miss a thing, from the ruffled auburn hair to the bare feet, and her wide-eyed scrutiny of what lay between them sent a wave of colour flooding into Stacie's face. She wanted to duck out of sight, hide the all too brief nature of that black silk pyjama top which the other woman's stare informed her was blatantly sexy.

'I'm just coming, Mother,' Nicholas Kinsella said tightly. He looked like a man trapped in an embarrassing situation and not liking it at all; a faint redness had come up in his face, but Stacie was too busy taking notice of the name he had used to think about that. She couldn't see any physical resemblance, his mother was very slender and fine-boned, a little shorter than Stacie herself, and her features didn't reflect any of Nicholas's formidable power.

'Nicholas, who . . .?' his mother asked, her gaze still riveted on Stacie.

He ignored the implicit question. 'I won't be a moment—go back to the others.'

'No wonder you seemed so taken aback when we arrived,' Mrs Kinsella remarked in sudden tartness. 'I wondered why you looked as if a bomb had just dropped. Why didn't you say that you had someone with you?'

'Mother, this isn't what you think. Miss Murray is . . . is . . .' His attempt at calm explanation faltered and he shifted his feet uneasily, as though not quite sure what to say.

Stacie's sense of humour had reasserted itself. She came down the stairs and held out her hand, smiling limpidly at Mrs Kinsella. 'I'm Stacie Murray,' she said, wide-eyed and innocent. 'Nicholas and I are . . . friends.'

'Yes, I see,' Mrs Kinsella said faintly, shaking hands with polite reluctance, but her eyes still pinned to the way Stacie was dressed. 'I'm sorry if we woke you, Miss . . .'

'Stacie, please. I'm a very informal person,' Stacie said with what she hoped would be taken for a coy giggle.

'I can see you are,' said Mrs Kinsella with a return of the tart tone.

'But you didn't wake us up, really—we were wide awake, weren't we, Nicholas? We haven't been asleep all night.' Stacie let her head tilt slightly so that it almost brushed his wide shoulder, her rich red curls trailing down his shirt sleeve, and flicked her eyes sideways.

Nicholas Kinsella looked at her with intense dislike in those icy grey eyes, but for some reason which she found very interesting he did not deny the impression she was deliberately giving. He merely smiled stiffly, his hard mouth drawn back in such a poor mimicry of a smile that it looked far more like a snarl.

'Run along back to bed, Stacie, I'll see you later,' he said, and she decided it might be wiser to do as he said. That look in his eyes made her reluctant to tease him any further, it warned that the repercussions might be uncomfortable when he did see her again.

'Okay,' she said pliably. 'Goodnight, Mrs Kinsella— it was so nice to meet you, what a pity I'm leaving in the morning, I would have enjoyed having another chat with you.'

'You're leaving tomorrow?' Mrs Kinsella sounded relieved, which wasn't very flattering, but Stacie could understand her feelings.

'Yes, I have to go, don't I, Nicholas?' she cooed, meeting his eyes and daring him to deny it. He obviously didn't want to tell his mother that he was keeping her a prisoner in the house, so how was he going to get out of this?

'We'll see,' he muttered through his teeth, his hand gripping her arm and urging her towards the stairs, with a force she didn't like to challenge.

Stacie paused as she got to the second stair, a new idea occurring to her. She bent over the balustrade and brushed her lips across his mouth, feeling him stiffen.

'Don't be too long,' she whispered in an inviting voice, then ran upstairs with a broad smile, aware that they were staring after her in total silence. It wasn't until she was out of sight that Mrs Kinsella spoke, and then Stacie halted to listen with amusement.

'Nicholas, are you out of your mind? What is that girl doing here? You've got to get rid of her—I want her out of this house first thing tomorrow morning, do you hear?' She stopped speaking, but not to allow her son to say anything, merely to draw breath for a new outburst that made Stacie listen even more intently.

'What if Marianne had seen her? Nicholas, that girl has to go before Marianne gets up tomorrow—it would ruin everything!'

'You shouldn't have sprung this on me,' he said tersely, sounding like a man at the end of his tether. 'Walking in here out of the blue—it was stupid, what on earth possessed you? Why didn't you ring, warn me? Why didn't you stay in London for the night and give me time to make some sort of preparations instead of flying to London and driving on here right away?'

'Marianne was eager to see you, she wanted to surprise you,' Mrs Kinsella said plaintively. 'It was her idea, she insisted on coming straight here from the airport. If I'd had any idea that you had a girl with you, I wouldn't have let Marianne talk me into it.'

Who was Marianne? Stacie wondered with a stupid little stab of jealousy. His girl-friend? He wasn't married, was he? That idea sent a wave of scarlet flowing up into her face, her hands screwed up into fists and she bit her lip to stop herself from making a sound.

'A pity you did,' Nicholas muttered, and his mother sounded angry as she answered him.

'Well, how was I to know? You told me it was only business that was keeping you here. I'd have insisted on staying the night in London so that I could ring you and warn you that we were coming if I'd had any notion what we'd find.'

'The whole plan was damned stupid,' Nicholas said grimly. 'Flying all this way . . .'

'It seemed a good idea to me. When you said on the phone that you couldn't get back until after Christmas, Marianne said what a pity it was and what fun it would be to come over and surprise you—a sort of Christmas present. She thought it would be exciting to spend Christmas in England. This house sounded so tranquil and lovely; it would make a wonderful place for Christmas, it seemed such a marvellous idea.' Mrs Kinsella sighed heavily. 'And now I wish I'd stayed in Boston!'

She couldn't wish it more than Stacie did, although that was stupid, too, because Nicholas was going to have to let her leave the house now. He couldn't keep her here while his mother and this unknown Marianne were around. Stacie told herself she was eager to see the back of him, she couldn't wait to get away, but somehow she felt no ring of conviction in the thought. Was Marianne beautiful? she wondered. Not that it was any concern of hers, of course; nor did she care one way or the other, but she would like one look at the other girl, she couldn't help being curious about her.

'Did your talks go well?' Mrs Kinsella asked, and Nicholas sounded abstracted as he answered.

'They were tougher and took longer than I'd expected, but I think they were successful. I can't tell you any more about them yet. I told you, they were secret talks and for the moment they have to stay confidential. As soon as I can, I'll tell you all about them.'

'Did you have that girl here all the time?'

Nicholas gave an exasperated sigh. 'I don't want to talk about her.'

'I'm sure you don't. Really, Nicholas—a girl like that!'

Like what? Stacie thought, bristling with offence. Mrs Kinsella's voice had been loaded with distaste, and Stacie didn't like being talked about like a street-walker. It was bad enough to know that Nicholas Kinsella thought she was easy game, without hearing his mother taking the same line.

'Drop the subject, Mother,' Nicholas ordered sharply.

'I just don't understand you don't you love Marianne? She's such a beautiful girl, such a nice girl ... how can you do this to her? Nicholas, you know I've never interfered . . .'

'Then don't do it now,' he interrupted.

'Don't speak to me like that, Nicholas! I won't stand for it. You may order your staff around, but you aren't doing it to me. I'm your mother!'

Stacie could see where he had got it from; that high-handed, domineering manner that rode over anything that got in his way. Mrs Kinsella obviously didn't like having it turned on her, but she was capable of giving back whatever she got, and Stacie wasn't sorry to hear Nicholas being put in his place.

'Go back to the others and tell them I'm making sure that their rooms are ready for them,' Nicholas said in a deadly quiet voice. 'I won't be long. Did Roughton bring the drinks and sandwiches?'

'Yes,' his mother said reluctantly. 'Tony's eating all the sandwiches—he's always hungry. I can't understand how he stays so thin; it isn't fair. I'm on a permanent diet, you know I don't eat enough to keep me alive, yet if I eat a peanut it shows on the scales.' She sighed. 'Poor Marianne only wanted some hot milk. It was such a cold drive; the car heater didn't work properly, although the chauffeur refused to admit it. I was frozen by the time we arrived. Do you think we're going to have snow?'

'Go and drink some brandy by the fire, that will warm you,' Nicholas said with impatience.

'Promise that that girl will have gone in the morning?' Mrs Kinsella asked coaxingly, and Stacie heard the harsh intake of Nicholas's breath. 'Please, Nicholas! How can you do this to Marianne? I never thought I'd say this to you, but I'm ashamed of you— I'm not old-fashioned or a prude, you know that, I know the moral climate has changed beyond recognition in modern times—anything goes, that's what they say, isn't it? Oh, I can see that that girl's attractive, in a certain way—you think she's very sexy, I suppose, although I've never been able to understand what men see in girls of her type. Red hair is so blatant, and I'm sure she dyes it; it didn't look natural to me, and as for that black thing she was wearing . . . well, I couldn't believe my eyes. Who would wear something like that?'

'I would,' Nicholas said shortly, and his mother gasped. 'She was wearing a pyjama top of mine.'

'Nicholas!'

'I lent it to her because she didn't have any nightclothes with her,' Nicholas said succinctly.

'I suppose I should be grateful she was wearing anything at all!' his mother snapped furiously.

'Mother, you're jumping to conclusions. I can't explain, but you're upsetting yourself over nothing; it isn't important.'

'At least you have enough sense to know that,' Mrs Kinsella said sharply. 'That's how I'd describe her—of no importance whatever. I'm glad to hear you say so.'

Stacie had heard enough; she turned and made her way back to her own room and bolted herself securely into it. The moon had risen and was making cold, swirling patterns on the ceiling and walls, the wind howled like a wolf around the house, cried in the trees and along the gutters. Stacie lay down on the bed and closed her eyes, feeling cold and angry. She hated Nicholas Kinsella and his mother: and tomorrow he was going to have to let her leave this house or she would make him regret it!

CHAPTER FOUR

STACIE woke up to find the room full of cruel sunlight that streamed across the bed and made her eyes wince; she had a headache, she discovered, no doubt due to the hours of sleep she had lost last night, and as she threw back the covers and staggered to the window to stare across the wintry landscape she remembered all the reasons she now had for hating Nicholas Kinsella, and her headache grew worse. She leaned on the sill, cursing the sunlight; it was as deceptive as a man, glittered brightly but had no warmth. The sky was clear and pale, the wind had dropped and there were no clouds, but Stacie was not surprised, when she opened the window, to find the air icy. She closed the window again and went to shower. At least that would wake her up and might even clear this headache.

She dressed hurriedly, listening for some sound in the house which would betray that someone else was awake. The new arrivals would probably sleep quite late; when she looked at her watch she found it was almost ten o'clock, and wondered: what time would they have breakfast? She sat down in front of the dressing-table to brush her hair and put on some make-up; she wasn't meeting the unknown Marianne without her warpaint! If Mrs Kinsella approved of the girl, Stacie could be certain she wasn't going to like her. She had the feeling she would never see eye to eye with Mrs Kinsella about anything.

Before she went to the door she collected her small clutch purse and her camera from the chair on which they lay. With any luck she would never see this room again; after breakfast she might be allowed to leave. She took a last look around it; admitting reluctantly that it was a very pretty room and very luxuriously furnished. A pity she remembered so vividly what had happened here last night—and, even more painful, what had almost happened. A small, rapid, pulse beat at the base of her throat and her face ran with angry colour. She still couldn't understand how she could have lost her head like that, but she despised Nicholas Kinsella. He had made that pass at her knowing he had another commitment. A wife? Was he married to this Marianne? He was an opportunist, unscrupulous, amoral—and she loathed herself for letting him touch her.

Turning away, she unbolted the door, but as she turned the handle a jab of alarm went through her. What if Nicholas Kinsella had come along here during the night and locked the door? It wouldn't surprise her; in fact it would be typical. His mother had tried to get him to promise that Stacie would leave next day, but Stacie couldn't remember hearing him agree.

The door creaked open, though, and she gave a sigh of relief. She moved softly down the corridor, listening. Her foot was still painful, her limp pronounced, she couldn't do up her sneaker because of the bandages; it hadn't been easy to get her foot into her sneaker, let alone tie the laces.

She looked down into the hall and saw Roughton sitting on a chair near the front door, reading a newspaper. Stacie had been so quiet that he hadn't heard her, the paper rustled as he turned a page and she bit her lip. Now what?

From the landing two corridors spread out, one on each side, and Stacie already realised that the rooms along her corridor were empty; their doors stood ajar and as she passed she had looked into each one and seen immaculate, unoccupied rooms. This was a very large house built on three floors, there must be more than a dozen bedrooms and judging by those she had been glancing at they were all beautifully furnished. It must be the perfect place for a private business conference of limited size; no doubt Nicholas Kinsella offered total security and peaceful surroundings to the firms he met here to discuss big deals. No hotel could promise complete security.

She looked down the other corridor. The new arrivals must have been given rooms along there; were they all asleep? Or had they already gone down to have breakfast? They couldn't have got to bed before four in the morning, the most probable thing was that they were still fast asleep, and Stacie wanted them around when she next saw Nicholas Kinsella. She had to get away from here, and he couldn't refuse to let her leave if his mother was listening. Mrs Kinsella's arrival had handed Stacie a weapon she fully intended to use. If Nicholas could be ruthlessly opportunist, so could she.

She crept back to one of the empty bedrooms and sat down on a chair out of sight of the door. Sooner or later she would hear someone on the stairs. As long as it was neither Nicholas nor Roughton she could then come out of hiding, and join the newcomer. With any luck, if Nicholas should come looking for her, he might not think of peering behind the door of each room. He would imagine she had gone downstairs and look for her there. If he did find her, she would have to start screaming the place down, bring his mother scuttling out to see what on earth was happening. His reluctance, last night, to explain to his mother what Stacie was doing in the house had been very revealing.

She almost fell asleep on the chair, she was still so tired, but some fifteen minutes later she came bolt upright as she heard movements. A door closed along the other corridor. Stacie heard footsteps and got up. She was certain it wasn't Nicholas; she was beginning to recognise the sound of his firm strides. She went out and looked anxiously at the landing, just as the young man walking across it turned his head in her direction. Stacie saw the surprise in his face and sagged with relief. She didn't know who he was, but she was sure he wasn't one of Nicholas's security men. He wasn't dressed like one, his face didn't have that tough impervious alertness.

'Well, hi!' he said, smiling at her. 'I thought I'd be the only one around so early.' Stacie noted the American accent and the smooth olive-gold tan, and wondered if he was the Tony Mrs Kinsella had talked about last night, the one who was always hungry. He had halted and was waiting for her, so Stacie hurried over to join him, smiling back.

'Hallo, I'm Stacie—you must be Tony.' She mentally crossed her fingers as she said that with casual confidence, watching his thin tanned face. He was in his early twenties, she decided; very tall and thin with long slim legs and a small waist, he seemed to be flat all the way down, but he moved with grace and ease, like a dancer.

'That's right,' he said, studying her with curiosity. She saw his eyes on the camera hanging around her neck and grinned.

'I'm a photographer from the *Globe*,' she said, and Tony's thin black brows shot up. He had a Mediterranean colouring, thick black curls cut very short, dark brown eyes and that olive skin; Stacie had seen many young men who looked like Tony when she was on holiday in Europe. But who was he? she wondered. Why was he here with Mrs Kinsella and the unknown Marianne? Could he be Marianne's brother?

'You don't say?' he murmured, looking incredulous. 'Are you here to take pictures of Nicholas?' He sounded as if he expected the answer to be in the negative.

Stacie looked at him wryly. 'Yes,' she said with conscious amusement. Well, it was true enough, although not in the sense he had meant it. He must suppose that Nicholas had given her permission to take pictures.

'Good grief, I don't believe it. He never—but never—allows the press to take pictures of him.' Tony surveyed her closer, with more interest, his eyes wandering from her rich dark red hair, the full, gleaming coils of it touched into brilliance by the cold morning sunlight, over her face with riveted attention which noticed everything; the slanting green eyes with their curling lashes, the finely modelled nose and that full, moist red mouth. Tony's eyes were bright with amusement as he added: 'Obviously you impressed him more than photographers usually do.'

Stacie heard the undertones, she knew what he was implying and it wasn't that her work was exceptional, but although she resented his hint she gave no sign of it.

'Thank you,' she said limpidly. 'Were you on your way down to breakfast?'

'Yes, I'm famished—cold weather always makes me hungry. You coming down?'

'Yes, I'm hungry too,' said Stacie, falling into step and Tony glanced down at her feet.

'Why the bandages? Hurt yourself?'

'Sprained my ankle.' Stacie concentrated on Tony, aware that Roughton had risen as he saw her coming down the stairs. He folded his newspaper and put it down, frowning. Out of the corner of her eye Stacie watched him, wondering if he would try to stop her.

'How did you do that?' asked Tony. Roughton was listening; Stacie nerved herself to look his way, her face coolly offhand. He looked solid and watchful, but he wasn't moving, she saw from his eyes that he didn't quite know how to act, he didn't like to intercept her under Tony's gaze, but his stare held irritation and annoyance. Stacie decided to give him a big smile.

'Good morning, Roughton,' she said brightly. 'Isn't it a lovely day for the time of year?'

Roughton made a noise like a dying bullfrog, and dragged a wooden smile into his face. She thought he was agreeing and walked on after Tony.

As Tony opened a door at the other end of the hall he said to her: 'Have you been staying here? You seem to know your way around better than I do.' Stacie could see that he was consumed with curiosity about her. 'How long have you been here?' he asked.

She shot a look around the room they were entering. It was empty except for the pale sunlight which fell on heavy silver on the breakfast table and glittered, The room was panelled in golden oak in the regular lozenges of linenfold panelling; a few pictures hung around the walls, oils of anonymous landscapes dark with age, and several portraits of heavy men in eighteenth-century costume, one on a bay horse held by a groom, the other seated behind a desk in a room that looked very much like the one Stacie stood in at that moment.

'It seems like weeks, but I only arrived yesterday.' said Stacie, watching Tony dart greedily to the long mahogany sideboard to investigate the contents of the fluted silver dishes arranged along it. Tony lifted cover after cover, gloating.

'I love your English breakfasts,' he told her over his shoulder, helping himself to a little from all the dishes. 'Are you a good photographer? Hell, that's a stupid question—you must be, or your paper wouldn't have sent you and Nicholas wouldn't have let you in the gates.'

Stacie sat down and poured herself some of the fresh orange juice she found in a vacuum jug. It was icy cold and delicious when she sipped it.

'Will the rest of your party be down for breakfast?' she asked as Tony sat down opposite her and poured himself some juice.

'I doubt it—Marianne was just plain exhausted when she went to bed, and my mother never gets up for breakfast.' He forked some sausage into his mouth.

Stacie stiffened, her eyes on him. She had to bite back the words of disbelief that almost escaped. His mother? That meant he must be Nicholas's brother! But he looked nothing like him, although he had hair the same colour. Everything about him was totally different; his build, his facial structure, his eyes and his lively, casual manner. It had never even entered her head that Tony could be a Kinsella, he didn't have the powerful, dominating masculinity of his brother or his formidable presence, but then was that so surprising? Tony was the young brother and he must have grown up in the shadow of Nicholas, which couldn't have been easy for him.

Tony was unaware of the shock he had given her. He got on with his breakfast without looking up. Stacie reached for a fresh, warm roll kept hot in the folds of a damask napkin. She split it, buttered it lightly and spread it with marmalade.

'If you want toast, there's some sliced bread and a toaster on the sideboard,' Tony pointed out, watching her.

'The roll is fine, thanks.'

'You don't eat much, either, I suppose,' he said, picking up the heavy silver coffee pot and pouring himself some coffee. 'I can't understand this obsession with dieting. Marianne's the same; doesn't eat enough to keep a bird alive and then complains because she feels tired.' He smiled to himself as he drank some coffee. 'She looks good on it, though, I'll say that.'

'I haven't met her yet,' Stacie said coolly. 'Is she pretty?' She badly wanted to know that, although she despised herself for being so curious about a girl she had never met and was unlikely to meet again once she left this house.

'Pretty?' Tony frowned down at his breakfast. 'I wouldn't call her pretty, no. Beautiful, maybe. Marianne's got something pretty special.'

Stacie couldn't ask too many questions or she might arouse his curiosity because she really knew too few of the answers. She didn't even know if Marianne was his brother's wife, she hadn't a clue about her, but Tony would expect her to know if she was here with Nicholas's permission, so she couldn't betray her ignorance, she had to maintain her assumed air of omniscience.

'How long are you staying?' asked Tony, getting up to walk over to the sideboard. He slid a slice of bread into the toaster and pushed down the lever. Stacie watched, admiring the graceful, unaware line of his long slim body. He posed without knowing what he was doing, his body fell into elegant lines instinctively. He was dressed casually, in a white sweater with a V-neck and a pair of well-pressed dark grey flannel pants which emphasised the length of those legs.

'I'm leaving this morning,' Stacie remarked with more optimism than truth, and Tony looked at her sharply.

'Really? What a pity.' He took the toast as it popped up and came back to the table with it on a clean plate. Stacie watched him spread butter and marmalade on it. 'I was hoping you'd be around for a couple of days,' he said without looking up. 'I've never met a pretty photographer before; most of the press photographers I've seen have been men.'

'There aren't many of us,' Stacie said drily. 'Picture editors tend to think it's a male job. In a crowd you need to be able to elbow your way to the front to get a good picture, and the men don't give way just because you're a woman. On the contrary, they're pretty ruthless about shoving you aside.'

Tony tilted his head, grinning at her. 'But you've survived?'

'I've learnt to be ruthless too,' said Stacie. 'I can stamp on a foot if I have to . . .'

He laughed. 'You don't look ruthless to me.'

'Look again,' Stacie said, and he leaned forward over the table to stare into her green eyes with intent probing, smiling.

The door opened behind them and they both looked round in surprise. The atmosphere in the sunlit room altered radically as Nicholas Kinsella walked forward. Stacie felt her body stiffen, her colour rise in hectic response to the hard, icy glare of his grey eyes. It was ridiculous to feel guilty, she had done nothing to be guilty about, yet his stare held such hostility that it was impossible to avoid a sense of guilt.

'Hi, Nick,' Tony said too loudly, his smile too artificially cheerful. 'Say your cook here does a fantastic breakfast, I haven't eaten like that in years.' Although he was talking fast he was looking distinctly uncomfortable under his brother's gaze and Stacie felt him shoot a look at her, his brows together, as if wondering what part she played in the frozen expression on Nicholas's face.

Nicholas sat down and picked up the coffee pot. 'If you've finished, you might go upstairs and see if Mother's up yet,' he said coldly, pouring himself a cup of coffee.

'Sure,' Tony said obediently, getting up. Did he always run when Nicholas commanded it? Stacie wondered, sure that he did. He hesitated, smiling, at her. 'Will I see you again later? You're not leaving right now, are you?'

'I'm afraid so,' she began, and Nicholas interrupted curtly.

'No.'

She turned her head to eye him furiously. 'Yes,' she said between barely parted lips. 'Unless, of course, you're going to let me take some more pictures, Mr Kinsella?' and her angry eyes taunted him, wondering how he would react. She was running risks, like a child walking along the edge of a pit full of snarling lions; it was alarming and exhilarating at one and the same time, and Stacie enjoyed seeing Nicholas briefly at a loss.

'You can take some of me any time, Stacie,' Tony said, laughing, then caught his brother's eye as Nicholas switched his stare from Stacie's face. Nervelessly Tony backed towards the door, his usual grace deserting him. 'Well, I hope you do stay, see you,' he mumbled, and fled.

Nicholas sipped his coffee, a hand tapping on the table in a way she remembered vividly from their first meeting. His eyes were narrowed; icy slits beneath his level black brows. Stacie's self-respect wouldn't allow her to admit she was frightened of him, but that stare of his was a threat, a pressure; she felt it on the back of her neck, sharp and glittering like the blade of an axe.

'What have you been saying to my brother?'

'Small talk,' she said vaguely, shrugging.

'About what?'

'I can't really remember; he mostly talked about breakfast, I think.'

'Why was he gazing into your eyes like a moonstruck schoolboy when I arrived?' asked Nicholas with a curl of his lips which had little humour and a great deal of irritation. 'Been flirting with him, had you? That can stop—and don't think for one second that I'm joking. I don't want you getting involved with my brother.'

Stacie's green eyes flared with defiance and insulted pride. 'Don't tell me that—tell him.'

'I'm telling you!' he said in a tone like the snap of a whip, and his hand came down flat on the table at the same time, the crash of the blow making her jump.

Her nerves clanged and quivered, but she struggled to hide it as she snarled back at him, 'I'm good enough for you to make a pass at, but not good enough for your brother—is that what you mean?' She let contempt run through her voice and saw a hard flush in his face but he met her stare without looking away.

'And another thing—why did you go through that poisonous charade in front of my mother, last night? How dared you . . .'

'You deserved it. Don't tell me it's the first time in your life that you've got what you deserved?' She smiled maliciously at the anger in his eyes. 'They say all new experience is good for us.'

'Don't push me too far, Miss Murray,' he said, almost hoarse with rage, the skin drawn so tightly over his face that she could see the sharp bone structure underlying it. He pushed away his coffee cup and stood up and moved round the table with a loping stride, the lethal prowl of the tiger, muscled and sleek, and Stacie's green eyes grew nervously alert, watching that approach, feeling the difference between them as she had felt it last night when he made love to her and her own warm, vulnerable, yielding flesh grew aware of his power and threat.

Bending over her, he spoke very softly: 'I'm a dangerous man to cross and you've already made me very angry. Don't get in my way again. I'm not altering my plans because of you. Until Nwanda gets back to his own country and makes the announcement there will be no leak on this side. You're not leaving here until I decide it's safe to let you go. Is that understood?'

Stacie swallowed. 'What will you tell your mother?' she asked pointedly.

'What you apparently just told my brother—that you're a newspaper photographer here to take pictures of the house.' His eyes pinned her to her chair. 'And you won't make any more trouble, Miss Murray; you won't flirt either with me or my brother, and you won't worry my mother with any more coy behaviour.'

'Coy?' Stacie repeated. 'I've never been coy in my life!'

He looked from her feline, witch-green eyes to the blaze of red hair lit by sunlight, his expression brooding. 'No,' he agreed. 'I used the wrong word. Just make sure I don't catch you play-acting again; you deliberately gave the impression . . .'

'That you'd just been making love to me?' she supplied as he paused and she saw his mouth tighten at this unanswerable question.

'I must have been out of my mind,' he said. 'I was tired, I'd drunk too much wine.' He looked at her briefly, his eyes resting on her curved red mouth, then looked away. 'I'm human. Any man seeing you like that would have been tempted; you should have stayed in your room, not gone wandering around in that silk top.'

Stacie laughed angrily. 'Oh, of course, it was all my fault—it always is the woman's isn't it?'

'Don't tell me you weren't aware of just how sexy you looked in that black silk!' he accused. 'I ought to have locked you in your room all night, it would have been a damned sight safer.' He moved away abruptly, his voice dropping, and went to lean against the window, his back to her. 'I shall explain to my mother that you're here to take pictures of the house, you can wander outside and go through the motions.'

'You stole my boxes of film!'

Nicholas sighed impatiently. 'You can have them back, take as many pictures outside as you like—before you leave you can give me back the films. I'll have them developed and send you the best ones of the house. You're not getting any pictures of me or my family, though, so don't waste your film trying to snatch some, because if won't do you any good.'

'Not even one of you and Marianne?' Stacie asked maliciously, and heard the harsh intake of his breath before he turned his head slowly to survey her with dislike.

'I suppose you got that out of Tony?'

Stacie didn't answer; she wasn't confessing that she had hovered at the top of the stairs last night, eavesdropping on his conversation with his mother. She shrugged and smiled, trying to outstare him.

'I'll kill Tony—he never could learn when to talk and when to hold his tongue,' said Nicholas with biting irritation, and Stacie felt a pang of sympathy for the unfortunate Tony, but in a contest between her own self-preservation and that of someone else, she felt she took precedence. There wasn't likely to be any painful repercussions for Tony; she wasn't so sure about herself. Nicholas Kinsella was a hard man, and he had influence, she should remember that.

'Does he work for you?' she asked to distract him, and he smiled coldly.

'Didn't you find that out from him? Well, there's no reason why you shouldn't know—yes, he works for my main company.'

'Doing what?'

'What he's told,' said Nicholas with a clarity that made her even more sorry for his brother, her sympathy spurring her into retorting.

'I like him; he's very sweet,' although she wished that didn't make Tony sound like someone totally negligible, and from Nicholas Kinsella's dry smile she could see that her comment had merely amused him. To improve Tony's image she added quickly: 'He's very good-looking.' It was true: Tony had a handsome face marred only by that undeniable pliability, a desire to please which one certainly did not read in Nicholas's self-willed features.

'Stay away from him,' Nicholas told her at once. 'He's too impressionable; ever since he left school he's been in love with one unsuitable girl after another, he has no sense where women are concerned.'

The door opened and Mrs Kinsella arrived in a sweet

cloud of perfume; floral, lingering, it immediately filled the room. 'There you are, Nicholas,' she said, but she was looking at Stacie without warmth. 'Good morning, Miss Murray—are you just leaving?'

'Miss Murray has to stay on another day to take some more pictures,' Nicholas put in before Stacie could answer.

'Pictures?' his mother repeated blankly.

'Of the house. Didn't I tell you last night? Yes, she's a photographer from the *Globe*, one of the leading British newspapers. I promised to let them have some pictures. There was some concern about an American buying another of their stately homes, they want to make sure I'm not destroying anything, and to set their minds at rest I agreed to let them send a photographer here.'

Mrs Kinsella looked disbelieving. 'You never mentioned it last night.'

Stacie opened her purse and produced her wallet. She hunted out her newspaper security pass and showed it to Mrs Kinsella without a word. The other woman stared at it, a frown creasing her forehead.

'I see.' Her eyes lifted coldly. 'So you hardly know my son.'

'I only met him yesterday,' Stacie told her with blithe disregard for the distasteful accusation in her face. She found that thought astonishing, herself; she felt like adding: 'He's a fast worker,' but she decided to forgo the pleasure of seeing Mrs Kinsella blench.

'I don't understand the world today,' Mrs Kinsella said with apparent irrelevance, except that Stacie perfectly understood what she meant, and wished suddenly that she hadn't been in such a mischievous mood last night. She could hardly blame Mrs Kinsella for having an impression of her that she herself had gone to some lengths to give.

'If you've finished your breakfast,' Nicholas said to

her drily, 'perhaps you'd like to start work.' He picked
up her camera from the sideboard, where she had left it,
and held it out to her, his grey eyes pointedly sardonic.
He didn't have to rub it in, she thought rebelliously. It
was all his fault, and she didn't like getting horrified,
censorious looks from his mother even if she had
brought them on herself.

'I shall need my films,' said Stacie, slipping the strap
of her camera over her head just as the door opened
again and a girl came into the room. Stacie knew who
she was, of course, before Mrs Kinsella said her name.

'Marianne dear, there you are—come and sit down
and have some coffee with me.' Mrs Kinsella picked up
the pot and felt it, frowning. 'Oh, it's cold—Nicholas,
would you ring for some more?'

He nodded, then looked at Stacie. 'Come along, Miss
Murray, I'll get Roughton to take you on a tour of the
grounds.'

Marianne was staring at her curiously. Mrs Kinsella
said hurriedly: 'Miss Murray is a photographer from a
British newspaper, dear.'

'Oh, have you come to take some pictures of
Nicholas?' Marianne asked, smiling at Stacie. She was
slight and fair, with fine blonde hair that hung in a
straight silky curtain around her face, a pale skin and
grave dark blue eyes. There was something calm and
still about her, a little childlike; Stacie decided she was
faintly anaemic, lacking in colour, but she had the sort
of ethereal beauty one saw sometimes in medieval
paintings. She looked as if she should have a unicorn's
head in her lap.

'No, she's only here to take pictures of the house,'
Nicholas told her.

'Mr Kinsella is camera-shy,' Stacie murmured, and
got a look from him which promised reprisals later.

Marianne laughed. 'It isn't easy to have your picture
taken, is it? I can never smile naturally. The minute I

see a camera pointing in my direction my whole face sets like concrete.'

'I think most people feel like that,' said Stacie, admiring the white jersey wool dress the other girl was wearing. It was beautifully styled and the tiny scarlet buttons and matching belt gave Marianne the colour she otherwise lacked. She had the slender figure of a boy, her breasts tiny and her hips narrow.

'If you're ready, Miss Murray?' Nicholas said with polite impatience, holding the door in a pointed manner. Stacie was staring at Marianne's hands which lay on the table. Marianne wasn't wearing a wedding ring. She wasn't wearing a ring of any kind, her small pale hands were quite bare.

CHAPTER FIVE

NICHOLAS walked down the hall to where Roughton had sprung to his feet at the first sight of his employer, and Stacie followed, ruefully realising that she was going to have Roughton for her guide of the estate, and wishing she could get out of this tour, because what good was it going to do her if Nicholas Kinsella was going to destroy the photographs she took before he let her leave this damned house? She increasingly wished she had stayed in Helen's house and not come over here to investigate her suspicions. In future she would let William do his own reporting. This would never have happened to him, or, if it had, he wouldn't have found himself trapped in such a worrying emotional tangle.

'Roughton, take Miss Murray on a tour of the house and park—outside. Take your time, don't hurry, let her take as many pictures as she likes, but don't let her ask you any questions and whatever you do, don't lay a hand on her. Is that understood?'

Looking worried Roughton stared back at him. 'Yes, sir.'

'Not a hand on her,' Nicholas repeated grimly, and Stacie didn't know if Roughton found him alarming, but she certainly did when he looked like that: black brows straight and frowning, eyes hard, mouth a tight line.

Roughton swallowed. 'No, sir.'

Nicholas nodded. 'Don't forget that unless you want to find yourself facing a charge of sexual assault from her and dismissal from me.' He said the sentence so quietly that for a moment Roughton just looked blank—and then his eyes bulged and he opened his mouth as if to say something, utter a protest, Stacie

74

could see the amazement and indignation in his face and waited for him to say something, but as he met Nicholas's cold eyes he closed his mouth again and didn't speak.

'I'll get you that film,' Nicholas said to her, walking away towards the door of the study in which he had interviewed her the day before.

As he walked into the room Roughton looked down at her and Stacie gave him a propitiating smile, feeling guilty because she had exaggerated her reaction to the way he had carried her across the park yesterday.

'What's that all about?' he growled under his breath. 'What've you been saying about me?'

'Nothing,' said Stacie with another coaxing smile. She didn't want to spend an hour or so walking around the grounds with a sulky Roughton, he was hardly charming at the best of times. When he was offended he would probably be very bad company indeed.

Unappeased, Roughton scowled. 'You'd better not. I'm not losing this job for you or anyone,' and then stopped talking as Nicholas came back with his hands full of her yellow boxes of film. Nicholas looked from one to the other of them, eyes probing, but Roughton had turned back to wood and was staring at a point just above Stacie's head, so Nicholas looked back at her, handing her the films.

'Better get your jacket on,' he said. 'Roughton, fetch it for her, will you?'

As Roughton walked away Stacie said tartly: 'You searched my car, I gather.'

Nicholas didn't deny it or apologise.

'Don't apologise,' she said with a sudden return of anger. 'You ought to see a shrink about your condition, it could get worse.'

'Now what are you talking about?' he asked wearily. 'Athough maybe I shouldn't ask—I don't suppose for a second that I'm going to like the answer.'

'You're suffering from megalomania—if you look it up in the dictionary you'll find it means delusions of grandeur . . .'

'I know what it means,' he said, staring at her as if he thought it was Stacie who was slightly round the bend—and maybe he was right, it wouldn't be surprising after the last twenty-four hours. Stacie had always had a high level of energy, a strong sense of her own identity and a comforting ability to bounce back after a crisis; if she hadn't been tough-minded she would never have survived in her job. It wasn't a job for ladies who swooned at the slightest threat. But since she first drove up to the gates of this house she had found herself whizzing from one shock to another and it hadn't stopped yet; she barely had time to adjust to one realisation before another hit her. That was calculated to scramble the best brains.

'What was Roughton saying to you when I came back?' Nicholas asked, taking her by surprise. 'Was he threatening you?'

Stacie wasn't going to get the unfortunate Roughton into any more hot water. 'No,' she said. He had only been a weapon she used to get back at Nicholas Kinsella and she didn't want to lose the man his job. Stacie had a sense of fair play which made her uneasy if she ignored it; no doubt Roughton was well paid and no doubt he needed the money. It wasn't easy to get good jobs these days, when you did find one you tended to hang on to it; although Stacie couldn't see why anyone wanted to go around with a gun threatening people, surely Roughton didn't enjoy it? But he probably loved it, she admitted wryly—it probably gave him a terrific kick and made him feel important. He was right, in one way; having a gun in your hand certainly makes people look at you in a respectful way. You weren't likely to be ignored, at any rate.

Roughton reappeared with her jacket, still looking

sulky, and Nicholas took it from him and held it out to
her. Stacie slipped her arms into it, feeling him standing
behind her so close that she could hear him breathing,
and wishing she was not so desperately conscious of
him. If she wasn't very, very careful she was going to
fall in love with him—and that would be disastrous,
because there could be no future in it, it would be one
of those messy tangles which leave you with nothing but
pain and a big dent in your self-respect. When he
walked away he would be going back to Marianne.
Stacie had seen her now, she knew Marianne was the
sort of girl he would marry; a classy girl who would fit
into his world like a round peg into a round hole.
Marianne was perfect for him, you could see she had
had money all her life, she had been sheltered and
watched over and protected. She hadn't had to earn her
own living or look after herself in a big city where the
nights could be dangerous and the days packed with
tedium. Stacie could almost hear herself becoming
damp with self-pity as she thought how easy life must
have been for Marianne and how hard it had been for
herself.

'Sure you can manage to walk on that foot?' asked
Nicholas with sudden hesitation, and Stacie looked
down at her bandaged ankle, the untied sneaker with
the laces removed so that she wouldn't trip over them.
She was tempted to look plaintive and helpless; no
doubt that would be what Marianne would do—and it
was a clever trick, making a man feel protective; it
made him feel good, too, it bolstered his own ego.
Stacie wouldn't do it, though, not this time. If she
hadn't known her own reasons for being tempted to do
it she wouldn't have hesitated. Stacie knew how to act
when the occasion arose, she could flutter her lashes
and smile when what she really wanted to do was
scream, but it was one thing to act like that for practical
reasons and quite another to do it because you wanted

a man to stay with you and not walk back to another woman. That, Stacie felt, was despicable, and she wouldn't do it.

'It doesn't hurt so much today,' she said honestly, instead.

Nicholas smiled, the hard angles of his face surprisingly warm. 'I told you it wasn't broken—but you knew that, didn't you? You were trying to pull the wool over my eyes. You'll have to get up earlier in the morning to do that.'

'I'll stay awake all night if necessary,' Stacie retorted, and he laughed.

'I believe you would.' He opened the front door. 'Don't give Roughton any trouble, will you? It won't do you any good, you know. You couldn't get out of the gate; there's a man in the lodge and the gates are electrically operated from the house.'

'Roughton's my keeper more than my guide, is he?' she asked without needing an answer, and Nicholas lifted his broad shoulders in a shrug. This morning he was wearing very casual dress, a white shirt under a black cashmere sweater which was obviously very expensive, smooth black pants which made his legs look even longer than usual. His skin was freshly shaved and his hair brushed down, a stray strand wandering down over his forehead, as the wind blew into his house.

'It's cold out there,' said Stacie, shivering, stuffing the boxes of film into her jacket pockets.

Nicholas turned up her collar for her so that it framed her face. 'Off you go,' he said remorselessly.

'You're a heartless brute,' she accused, and he grinned.

'You're starting to know me.'

That wasn't so funny because she *was* beginning to know him, and she liked what she was discovering far too much; she wished she liked him less. Hurriedly she reminded herself of all the reasons she had for hating

his guts, she remembered last night, his lovemaking and
then what he had said to his mother about her, what his
mother had said with such distaste and shame-making
contempt. Oh, she had a hundred reasons for detesting
Nicholas Kinsella, and as she walked around this
damned great pile of a house in the freezing cold wind
with his sullen henchman at her heels she was going to
count them all up and make sure she didn't forget a
single one of them.

She was irritated enough to exaggerate her limp as
she set off, but she heard the front door close,
nevertheless; Nicholas wasn't buying her act, he had
gone back into the house. Stacie buried her hands in her
pockets, hunched up in gloomy resistance to the wind
which knifed her through her thick jacket, and looked
up at the white walls of the house. A little quiver of
pleasure went through her at the elegance and restraint
of the proportions, the high flat windows and those
chastely classical pediments above them, the white stone
carved in perfect symmetry so that the window looked
as if it had slipped down out of the triangular envelope
above. There was no other ornament, the house was
solid and uncluttered. Who had built it? she wondered.
She knew nothing about Emberly Hall, for all she knew
it might be the work of some very famous architect.

'Are you going to give me a guided tour?' she asked
Roughton mischievously, glancing sideways at him, and
he looked aghast.

'Me? I don't know nothing about the place.' He
looked at it without admiration. 'Big as a barn and
twice as draughty,' he commented.

'How long have you worked for Mr Kinsella?' Stacie
asked, and he growled back, scowling again.

'He said no questions, and what he says he means.'
They turned the corner and Stacie halted in amazement,
seeing a lake below her, the cold grey water gleaming
like a frozen mirror under the winter sky. Along the

edge on the far side stood some trees whose branches moved in reflection on the water, as the wind blew them into bending arches. There were some dark green pines and cedars in the park, but most of the other trees were bare, stripped of their leaves long ago.

The parkland undulated softly on every side; cropped frost-stiffened grass sparkling in sunlight and a few sheep ambling under the trees some distance from the house, a tranquil winter landscape Stacie's eyes roamed over with curiosity.

'Aren't you going to take some pictures?' Roughton demanded.

'Why not?' Stacie put some film in her camera while he watched, and began to take pictures of the house, the lake, the sheep under the trees. When in a spirit of mischief she turned her camera towards Roughton he backed, putting his large hand over her lens.

'Here, what're you doing?'

'Say cheese,' Stacie mocked, and he glowered at her.

'I don't think that's funny.'

'You don't think anything's funny,' she observed. 'You haven't got a sense of humour, have you?'

'That's right,' he said with dogged refusal to smile. He was still offended by being told to keep his hands off her; he knew she had said something to Nicholas to prompt that order and Roughton resented it. Stacie considered coaxing him out of his sulks, but then remembered herself carried over his shoulder, the stinging slap of his big hand on her behind, and decided not to bother. It might teach him to keep his hands to himself in future.

A shout made them both turn to look along the side of the house. Tony was walking towards them from the back of the house. He was wearing a tan leather bomber jacket zipped up the front and gripping his thin waist tightly and his face had a healthy colour from the cold wind.

'Taking a stroll?' he asked Stacie as he joined them. 'Mind if I come? I'm bored out of my skull, there's nothing to do indoors.'

Roughton had the agitated look of the slow thinker who suspects he is being faced with a difficult decision without having a clue which of two choices to take.

'Er . . . does Mr Kinsella know . . .' he began, and Tony looked at him with amazement, raising his brows with an expression oddly like his brother's when Nicholas was angry.

'What?' he asked, and Roughton shuffled his feet without answering. Stacie watched thoughtfully Tony seemed different out here, away from his brother's looming presence, he had a carefree air, he was relaxed and sure of himself.

'Have you seen the swimming pool yet?' he asked Stacie, turning a cold shoulder on Roughton.

'No, is it an indoor pool?'

He nodded. 'Nicholas just had it built—it's round the back of the house, out of sight of the road. The building he used had been put up in the nineteenth century as a greenhouse; he had it altered structurally to fit in with the rest of the house, you'd hardly know it wasn't original and from outside you'd never guess it was a swimming pool.'

They walked slowly round the house and Roughton fell behind, although not so far that he couldn't hear their conversation, and Tony occasionally threw him an irritated look, conscious of him all the time. Roughton would repeat everything he heard to Nicholas and Tony didn't like having that reminder of his brother around him.

The swimming pool jutted out from the rest of the house in an octagon that had a certain style of its own. Tony halted at the door and looked back at Roughton.

'No need to come in—you can smoke a cigarette while I'm showing Miss Murray the pool.'

'Mr Kinsella said I wasn't to leave her alone,' Roughton protested.

'She won't be alone,' Tony pointed out. 'I'll be with her. What do you think she's going to do? Steal a towel?' He opened the door and waved Stacie through it, followed her and closed the door in Roughton's gloomy face. 'I get so sick of having those guys dog my heels,' he muttered, and the words echoed and rang in the building which had the hollow emptiness of a place rarely used. Stacie stared at the high, glass ceiling arching overhead, at the unreal blue of the water over which dappled light drifted and danced. Around the pool the floor was paved with blue and white tiles and at one end stood a row of cubicles, in front of which were arranged some padded loungers and a low whitewood table.

'Feel like a swim? There are some spare costumes in one of the cubicles in case guests haven't brought one of their own.'

Stacie looked down at her foot. 'I'd have loved a swim, but I don't think I'd better.'

Tony made a face. 'Sorry, I'd forgotten your ankle— how is it? How did you do it, by the way? You never told me.'

'I fell off a tree.'

He laughed, eyeing her with disbelieving speculation. 'You're pulling my leg.'

'No,' she said gravely.

'What were you doing up a tree? Rescuing a stranded kitten? Picking mistletoe?' Tony began to walk around the pool and she followed more slowly.

'I was taking pictures of this house.'

Reaching the loungers, Tony sat down on one and patted the one next to him. 'Take the weight off your foot.'

She wasn't reluctant to do so, she sank down with a sigh of relief. 'It does ache, actually; it's quite painful again.'

'Is your job always that dangerous?' Tony asked, lying back with his hands under his head, staring at the glass roof. The light filtering through the smoky glass had a strange, unearthly colour. 'What made you take up photography?'

'Pure accident,' Stacie told him. 'A local photographer came to my school to give us a talk about his job and he made it sound so fascinating that I decided to take a course at the local Polytechnic. I sold some pictures to London papers while I was working as a freelance and the picture editor on the *Globe* liked my work and offered me a job as a junior, so of course I jumped at it.'

'You must be good to be on a national paper,' Tony commented. 'I wish I was that good at something— anything! I wouldn't mind what! I'm just ordinary, though and with a brother like mine that's no joke. Nobody takes me seriously with Nick around. The last girl I dated turned out to be hoping to get to know Nick. The story of my life,' he added gloomily. 'Sooner or later they all flip over Nick.'

'You *are* feeling sorry for yourself,' Stacie said, half-smiling, but she did not doubt that he was right. Who would look twice at Tony if Nicholas Kinsella was around?

She was feeling irritated with herself because she had just let Nicholas off the hook. She had got up that morning fiercely determined to make him let her go, whatever she had to do to force his hand, and she had had a whole armoury of weapons to hand—his mother, Marianne, Tony. She could have carried on with the act she had played for Mrs Kinsella last night. She had intended to—Nicholas had bullied her into backing off and she hadn't quite had the nerve to defy him, there had been something about those cold grey eyes and that hard face which had made her think twice about risking his anger again. Now she was annoyed with herself.

How spineless could you get? What could he do to her, anyway?

'Try looking at it from my point of view,' said Tony, turning to look at her. 'How would you like to be in my shoes? Always playing second fiddle to Nick? I'm pretty sick of it, I can tell you. Just watch him! He always gets his own way with everyone.'

'Does he?' Stacie asked coolly, even more angry with herself for the way she had let Nicholas ride roughshod over her that morning. Tony was right, damn him, she wished she could deny it but she couldn't.

'Except with our mother,' Tony said carefully. 'She's the only one who can ever get him to do what she wants and she uses a water-dropping-on-a-stone technique. It makes him as mad as hell, but she often wears him down in the end, he gives in just to shut her up.' He paused, watching Stacie. 'That's why he's marrying Marianne.'

Stacie's eyes widened and she stiffened, listening intently. Had Tony forgotten who he was talking to? Or was he deliberately spilling the family secrets to her, to annoy his brother?

'Her mother was at school with ours, they've been friends ever since, and Mother's great dream has always been that Nick should marry Marianne. She's been feeding him the idea for years, and they've brainwashed Marianne into thinking she's in love with him.'

Stacie couldn't buy that. 'Did she need brainwashing?' she asked incredulously. Nicholas Kinsella wouldn't be so very hard to fall in love with—in fact, it would be all too damnably easy, he was more attractive than he had any right to be, given his other advantages. It wasn't fair for one man to be so showered with life's gifts. It encouraged him to be too arrogant and sure of himself; Nicholas Kinsella's ego needed to be deflated and Stacie wouldn't pass up a chance of pricking it, if one came her way.

'She's still very young for her age,' Tony said, and Stacie had to look away to hide a smile. Tony wasn't exactly mature, himself.

'I met her this morning,' she pointed out, in a soft voice.

'She's not very strong,' Tony said moodily—and that much Stacie did believe. The girl was beautiful but frail; she looked as though a puff of wind might blow her away, she did not look as if she could cope with Nicholas Kinsella's tough reality. But maybe that was what had attracted him? Opposites do attract, he might be drawn by Marianne's ethereal beauty simply because it was a million light years from his own nature, and the same might apply to Marianne's feelings for him. Nicholas was a strong man, and a girl like Marianne might find that irresistible.

'He won't make her happy,' said Tony, and the fierceness in his voice made Stacie jerk to attention, picking up the emotion in him and suddenly understanding it in a flash of intuition which left her startled and sorry for him. She hadn't seriously pitied him until that moment. It couldn't be easy to be Nicholas Kinsella's brother, and know you would always play second string to him, but on the other hand it wasn't as tragic as Tony wanted to believe. He could have worse problems than that. He could, for instance, be in love with the girl who was going to marry his brother. Now *that* was a bad problem, and Stacie looked at him with sympathy.

Tony had flushed but he was looking defiant, too. 'He doesn't love her,' he said with raw anger. 'He's only marrying her because it suits him and it will shut Mother up. Don't you see—she'll be unhappy once she realises the truth? Marianne's the sort of girl who needs to be loved and looked after, and Nicholas isn't going to do it. Oh, she'll have plenty of money and he'll give her anything she wants, but he won't give her what she really needs. She isn't his type; they aren't suited.' He was talking rapidly, excitedly, but somehow something didn't ring true.

Stacie caught the sideways flicker of his eyes, as though he was watching her for some reaction to what he was saying, and felt a jab of suspicion.

'Nicholas won't be happy, either,' said Tony. 'That doesn't bother me much, it obviously doesn't bother him or he wouldn't be marrying a girl he knows very well he doesn't love, so why should I waste time on worrying about it? But it's the truth.'

'Why are you telling me all this?' Stacie demanded. 'At the very least you're being very indiscreet. I work for a national newspaper—don't tell me you've forgotten that, because I don't buy it. You just handed me a story that any gossip column in the world would eat up—it's just the sort of scandal they love.'

'You wouldn't do that,' said Tony with maddening certainty, but he slid off the lounger and looked at his watch. 'We'd better get back to Roughton.'

'He's probably shot off to the house to tell your brother you're in here with me,' Stacie said, and he grinned.

'I wouldn't be surprised. He won't like that, will he?'

She was puzzled by his air of triumph. 'For someone who's just been complaining that he feels dominated by his brother, you're taking that very casually.'

'I've never had anything on him before,' Tony said cheerfully.

'And now you do?' What on earth was he talking about? Why was he grinning at her in that way?

'Oh, come on, you know he'll go spare if he thinks you've been flirting with me again,' he said, and Stacie halted in her tracks.

He stopped and grinned at her and she thought fast, staring at him, guessing wildly.

'I listened at the door after he'd sent me to see if my

mother was up,' he told her without any visible sign of guilt. 'It was a very interesting conversation and I wish I could have heard more of it, but Roughton came along to see what I was doing, so I pretended I'd been doing up my shoe and walked off. I already had my suspicions that there was something going on between you and Nick. Most girls just don't talk to him like that, they go all weak at the knees and agree with everything he says. It makes you sick. But you talked back to him, I could see you weren't scared. In fact, you were in quite a temper and not afraid to show it. That's why I eavesdropped, I wondered what you'd say when I'd gone, and when Nick started shouting because he thought you'd flirted with me then I knew I was on the right track. It was obvious even through the door that you'd got right under his skin.'

'You are out of your mind,' Stacie said slowly, spacing each word out as though she spun it from her own entrails. Her face was tight and hot, she knew she had flushed, and she knew Tony had noticed and was looking even more pleased with himself. Looking back over their talk since she met him coming round the house she saw that the change in him, the surprising new self-confidence with which he had talked to Roughton, had all sprung from his overhearing her talking to his brother. For the first time in his experience of Nicholas, Tony felt he had a weapon to use against him. Stacie wasn't so sure she liked being thought of as a weapon and she didn't want to get caught in the crossfire of this particular private war. There is no battle so vicious or so potentially lethal as the fight between members of a family, only a fool gets involved in anything like that, and Stacie was no fool.

'You don't kid me,' said Tony, still euphoric with certainty. 'Look at it this way, Stacie—we're on the same side. We both want the same thing, don't we?'

'I hadn't noticed,' Stacie said with force. 'What's that?'

'You know very well!' said Tony, grinning, and of course she did; he had spelt it out by now, far too clearly for her to have missed his meaning. Tony was under the impression that she was having an affair with his brother and would want to stop Nicholas's marriage, and he was delighted to have found an ally. He probably felt he hadn't a chance of doing anything alone, but that with Stacie to help, he might be able to drive a wedge between the other two.

'You're way off course,' she said to him. 'For the record, I am not an interested party, so don't try to drag me into whatever's going on between you and your brother.'

'I'm not as stupid as Nick thinks I am,' Tony told her, unabashed. 'Even before I did my bit of eavesdropping I was wondering about you two. The last press photographer who tried to take a picture of Nick got his camera smashed. Nick never lets the press within miles of him. Yet here you were, calm as a cucumber. Then I remembered his face when we arrived—he looked thunderstruck. Boy, it must have been a shock to him to see us! Especially Marianne . . .'

They walked out of the pool house and there was no sign of Roughton. Stacie wasn't surprised by that, but her heart sank. She didn't want another stormy scene with Nicholas; this whole situation was getting too complicated and she wanted out of it. Whenever you get mixed up with human beings life gets complicated; they're unpredictable and contrary and permanently doing things that cause trouble. Stacie thought with wistful yearning of the cheerful noise of her sister's household. By comparison with what was going on around her at the moment, Helen's family were a tribe of little white mice.

'Don't you understand, Stacie, if we join forces . . .' Tony began, and she cut him short with impatience.

'I don't want to know, all this is nothing to do with me. I'm leaving as soon as he lets me.'

Tony laughed, looking delighted, gleeful. 'Why should he stop you? If you're telling the truth and there's nothing going on between you?'

Stacie walked away as fast as she could manage on her injured ankle without answering that. What could she say? Tell him the whole story about Saul Nwanda? Explain that she was being held captive here until the embargo was lifted on the talks? Well, of course she could tell him the truth, but she had a distinct feeling that Tony wouldn't believe her, because that explanation wouldn't cover what he had heard through the door, she had a sinking feeling that Nicholas hadn't mentioned Saul Nwanda. His first angry outburst had been about Tony—an accusation that she had been flirting with him, and an overbearing statement to the effect that Nicholas wouldn't allow her to get involved with his brother. No doubt it had sounded to Tony like personal jealousy, and it must have given his ego a big boost to imagine that his brother was jealous of him, it was that belief that had put a sparkle into his eyes and a spring into his step. He was in for a rude awakening at some later stage, but that was his problem.

Before she reached the front door she saw Nicholas coming; her eyes misted in shock, he looked so big and black and menacing, and she knew he was in a temper from the way he came, so fast she almost thought he must be burning up the icy ground he was stamping over.

'Now look what you've done!' she said to Tony in a muffled wail. She ought to push him first, let him take the first impact of Nicholas's temper, following the old rule about saving women and children first. At this precise moment Stacie wasn't sure under which heading she qualified: she felt she should sign up under both, she felt distinctly childlike in the face of Nicholas Kinsella's rage.

'Get into the house—I'll talk to you later!' Nicholas snarled at his brother as he halted in front of them.

Tony made no attempt to obey, he merely moved closer to Stacie, putting an arm around her shoulders.

'What are you yelling about?' he asked aggressively. 'I've been showing Stacie the new swimming pool. Any reason why I shouldn't?'

'Roughton was taking her around the house. I'd given him his orders—you had no business countermanding them, and if you interfere like that again you'll regret it.' Nicholas was talking in a deep, harsh voice, staring at Tony with eyes that flayed him. 'You stupid fool, have you forgotten she's from the press? Anything you say to her is likely to turn up in a gossip column, and don't think she'd hesitate to use it because you've been stupid enough to confide in her. Whatever she's promised, she'll conveniently forget once she's got away from here.'

'That's not why you don't want me to be alone with her,' said Tony, sneering. 'You fancy her yourself, that's the real reason.'

Nicholas's face stiffened into a barbaric mask of fury, his skin stretched over his bones, his eyes glittering. He was so angry that for a moment he didn't speak and Stacie found his face quite terrifying, but Tony was too full of bravado to back away.

'You'd better make up your mind which of them you want,' he baited Nicholas with a gleeful malice which showed in his face and voice. 'You can't have them both. It's Marianne you're supposed to be marrying—stick to her and leave Stacie to me!'

Nicholas moved in a sudden, savage lunge, the wind raking his thick black hair away from his face as he swung his fist at his brother's laughing face. Tony fell backwards with a crash and landed in a sprawl on the icy ground, his arms flung wide as he tried to save himself.

'You bastard!' Stacie screamed, sinking to her knees beside Tony. Blood trickled from the corner of his mouth as she bent over him. He pushed her away as she tried to help him, and struggled up alone, one hand gingerly fingering his jaw. He looked in disbelief at his fingers as he saw the blood on them.

'Are you all right?' Stacie asked anxiously, and Tony looked dazedly at her, nodding. She turned to glare at Nicholas. 'You didn't have to do that!'

'You almost broke my jaw,' Tony said sulkily, getting to his feet.

'Never talk to me like that again,' grated Nicholas in a voice which was raw with anger. 'Never! Do you hear me? Especially not in front of strangers! Or next time I *will* break your jaw to teach you not to talk out of turn. Now get indoors and in future stay away from her.'

Tony's lip was beginning to swell, the skin dark red and puffy. His mouth moved in a bitter smile, but he walked slowly away with a bent head, looking abruptly much younger and lacking in any confidence. Stacie stared after him, angrily sorry for him, then turned her eyes towards Nicholas, hating him.

'Did you have to humiliate him like that? You know you're stronger than he is—you didn't have to prove it. You're contemptible! I've never seen anything so sickening in my life!'

Nicholas stiffened, listening without trying to interrupt, his face icy. When she stopped talking he stared at her for a long moment and she felt a tremor of fear running through her whole body. He radiated threat.

'You caused that scene,' he said at last. 'The whole thing was your fault. I warned you to stay away from my brother—he's too much of a fool to realise the dangers of talking too freely to someone like you. If you let him make love to you, the way you did with me, he'd be only too ready to believe you were as sweet as honey. I know Tony . . .'

'Do you?' Stacie interrupted bitingly. 'I doubt that. He hates your guts, did you know *that*?'

Nicholas shrugged. 'I'm not discussing my brother with you, and if you've been discussing me with him you'd be wise to forget everything he said to you. Try to print any of it and . . .'

'And what? You'll break my jaw, too?'

He looked at that moment as if he might well do that, his eyes black with rage, but after a moment he smiled with a cruel twist of the lips that made her back away instinctively.

'I'd have to use other methods with you, but they would be just as effective in making sure you learnt to hold your tongue,' he said, and Stacie was alarmed enough to turn and limp into the house without another word.

CHAPTER SIX

As Stacie walked into the house she saw a little tableau at the foot of the stairs. Tony, his face in profile, looking away from her, was frozen in motion, while Marianne delicately touched his swollen lip with one slender finger. Her face was fully visible to Stacie, and it wasn't hard to read—she had a coin of scarlet colour in each cheek and her grave blue eyes were shocked and angry. Neither of them was speaking.

Then the still life broke up as they heard Stacie's footsteps. Tony turned and ran up the stairs, and Marianne gave Stacie a hostile stare, her hands clenching by her sides.

'Tony's lip has split! I hope you're pleased with yourself. Does it give you a cheap thrill to watch men fighting over you?'

Stacie considered her face, frowning. 'What makes you think they were fighting over me?'

'Tony told me! He says you're ... that you and Nicholas ...' Marianne seemed to be having difficulty putting it into words, she was very flushed, her hands gestured wildly. 'You know what he told me, don't you? Is it true?'

Roughton came through a baize-lined door at the end of the hall and Marianne shot him a quick look, then went into a room behind her, muttering to Stacie: 'Come in here, I want to talk to you.'

Stacie followed slowly, getting a sulky look from Roughton before she shut the door behind her. She found herself in a room she had never seen before, a square drawing-room with a fine old Persian carpet on the floor and walls lined with watered pink silk that rippled in the sunlight. Overhead hung a chandelier, the pendant lustres tinkling like frozen ice in the draught of air she had caused as she closed the door. She looked around with pleasure; it was an elegant, charming room, and she wondered how much of the delicate eighteenth-century furniture was originally part of the furnishing of the house when it was built. The cream silk brocade curtains were new and she could see that the sofas and chairs had been re-upholstered, but the clawed feet supporting them had a faintly tarnished look, the gilding had worn off and had not been renewed, and they had made deep circles in the carpet pile.

Marianne stood beside a half-decorated Christmas tree in the corner by the window. She was watching Stacie and fingering a large silver foil star.

'Is it true? About you and Nicholas?' she asked, and Stacie hesitated, frowning.

'You shouldn't listen to Tony, he resents his brother, he's jealous of him.'

Marianne's flush deepened. 'You don't need to explain Tony to me, I've known him all my life.' Her voice was high with anger, she was looking at Stacie as though she disliked her intensely, which wasn't so surprising, but was her hostility on Nicholas's account, or was it Tony she cared about?

'Then you must have known Nicholas as long,' Stacie said drily. 'Why do you need me to explain him to you?'

Marianne didn't answer that, her lower lip drew in and she bit it with small white teeth, staring at Stacie. 'You've been flirting with Tony. That's why Nicholas punched him, Tony says—is it true? I'm asking you a simple question, why can't you give me a simple answer?'

'I'm not on trial, I don't have to answer any questions.'

'Don't you think I have a right to ask questions?'

Marianne stared at her accusingly, the silver star twisting and crumpling between her trembling fingers, she seemed unaware she held it.

'Not of me,' Stacie said flatly.

'Nicholas has asked me to marry him!'

'Then ask him your questions,' Stacie returned coolly, watching the ruined star flash as Marianne saw what she had done to it and threw it away with an impatient gesture.

'I can't! I'm afraid to . . .' Marianne sank down on the sofa nearby and clasped her hands in her lap.

'Afraid of him—or afraid of what he might tell you?' asked Stacie with a bitter curiosity. She picked up the star and smoothed it out carefully, then, while Marianne watched her in silence, clipped it on to one of the branches of the tree. It would never look the same again, but it glittered brightly among the dark green pine needles whose scent filled the room with nostalgic memories of other years. Staring at the other decorations, Stacie asked: 'Did you bring these with you or find them here?'

'Roughton went into the nearest town to get them early this morning,' Marianne told her in a polite little voice. 'Christmas wouldn't be the same without a tree and decorations.'

Stacie moved a branch and a glass bell rang with a tiny silver sweetness that set her teeth on edge and made her want to cry.

'Are you in love with Nicholas?' she asked without looking round.

There was a silence, then Marianne said: 'I don't know. I saw a lot of him in the summer and I thought I was, but he's been abroad for weeks now and . . .' She gave a nervous little laugh. 'Love isn't like a tan, is it? It doesn't start to fade once the sun has gone away?'

'Are you asking me—or telling me?' Stacie hesitated about sitting down beside her; her ankle was aching and

she didn't want to stand around any more, so she sat
down on the floor and put her knees up, her arms
around them and her chin on her jeans. 'I wouldn't
know much about love anyway, I'm not an expert on
the subject. My love affairs have always faded away,
not like a tan but like measles ... one minute I'm
red-hot and definitely infected—and the next there isn't
a sign of the disease ...'

'How old are you?' Marianne asked her, and Stacie
replied frankly. 'You're four years older than me,'
Marianne said. 'How often have you thought you were
in love?'

Stacie's brow wrinkled. 'At first? Between seventeen
and nineteen, every second week, I went to a mixed
sexes school and I knew a lot of boys, then I met
someone much older and thought I loved him for nearly
three months. It was one of those heaven-and-hell
relationships, I swung from one to the other without
ever really knowing why. He was a bastard, totally
selfish and self-obsessed. His biggest kick was knowing
he could make me cry, and when I finally realised that I
walked out on him. After that, I fell in love a lot less
easily and I saw the men a damned sight more clearly.'

Marianne laughed, then sobered. 'I don't know many
men. I went to a girls' school—I was a boarder, we
didn't get to meet many boys and we were watched
pretty carefully. Then I went to a school in Switzerland
for a year to learn some German and improve my
French. I met a few Swiss boys—but we weren't
allowed to date.'

She had been closely chaperoned and guarded, Stacie
thought, less because her parents were worried about
her virtue than because she was an heiress, no doubt.
She was like a pale flower grown in a hothouse, never
allowed to feel the wind or the hot caress of the naked
sun. Her future had been mapped out for her and the
adults around her had been too shrewd to use

Say Hello to Yesterday
Holly Weston had done it all alone.

She had raised her small son and worked her way up to features writer for a major newspaper. Still the bitterness of the the past seven years lingered.

She had been very young when she married Nick Falconer—but old enough to lose her heart completely when he left. Despite her success in her new life, her old one haunted her.

But it was over and done with—until an assignment in Greece brought her face to face with Nick, and all she was trying to forget. . . .

Time of the Temptress
The game must be played his way!

Rebellion against a cushioned, controlled life had landed Eve Tarrant in Africa. Now only the tough mercenary Wade O'Mara stood between her and possible death in the wild, revolution-torn jungle.

But the real danger was Wode himself—he had made Eve aware of herself as a woman.

"I saved your neck, so you feel you owe me something," Wade said. "But you don't owe me a thing, Eve. Get away from me." She knew she could make him lose his head if she tried. But that wouldn't solve anything. . . .

Your Romantic Adventure Starts Here.

Born Out of Love
It had to be coincidence!

Charlotte stared at the man through a mist of confusion. It was Logan. An older Logan, of course, but unmistakably the man who had ravaged her emotions and then abandoned her all those years ago.

She ought to feel angry. She ought to feel resentful and cheated. Instead, she was apprehensive—terrified at the complications he could create.

"We are not through, Charlotte," he told her flatly. "I sometimes think we haven't even begun."

Man's World
Kate was finished with love for good.

Kate's new boss, features editor Eliot Holman, might have devastating charms—but Kate couldn't care less, even if it was obvious that he was interested in her.

Everyone, including Eliot, thought Kate was grieving over the loss of her husband, Toby. She kept it a carefully guarded secret just how cruelly Toby had treated her and how terrified she was of trusting men again.

But Eliot refused to leave her alone, which only served to infuriate her. He was no different from any other man... or was he?

These FOUR free Harlequin Presents novels allow you to enter the world of romance, love and desire. As a member of the Harlequin Home Subscription Plan, you can continue to experience all the moods of love. You'll be inspired by moments so real...so moving...you won't want them to end. So start your own Harlequin Presents adventure by returning the reply card below. <u>DO IT TODAY!</u>

BUSINESS REPLY CARD

First Class   Permit No. 70   Tempe, AZ

POSTAGE WILL BE PAID BY ADDRESSEE

**Harlequin Reader Service
2504 W. Southern Avenue,
Tempe, Arizona 85282**

NO POSTAGE
NECESSARY
IF MAILED
IN THE
UNITED STATES

coercion—they had merely kept her away from danger until she was old enough to interest the right sort of man. Did Marianne know that?

'But you knew Tony,' she prompted, and Marianne laughed.

'Oh, Tony! Well, I'd known him always—he was like a brother, we grew up together and I'm very fond of him, but nobody takes Tony seriously, nobody ever has; he isn't serious about anything.'

Stacie again felt sorry for Tony. Realising what he had been up against for years, who could blame him if he felt aggrieved from time to time? Nobody likes being dismissed as too negligible to think about, it was enough to make the most peaceful man feel murderous.

'Then last summer I saw Nicholas again—I hadn't seen him for ages and I suppose I'd changed a lot and . . .' Marianne shrugged. 'We started dating and everyone was so delighted, my mother was over the moon.'

I'm sure she was, Stacie thought cynically—it must have been dream-come-true time for one and all, their long-cherished plan finally in operation and the princess about to marry the prince, with bells ringing and flags flying.

'I was sure it was love, it felt like it,' Marianne was saying wistfully. 'Whenever I saw him I felt breathless.'

Stacie knew that feeling, he had taken her breath away more than once in the last two days, but she wasn't going to tell herself it was love. It was an instinctive sexual reaction to a man whose masculinity was so powerful that it was a threat.

'And then he went to Europe. He kept saying he'd be back soon, but he never came home—now and then he was in New York or on the West Coast, but he never had time to fly to Boston to see us, he said he was up to his ears in work and . . .' Marianne sighed heavily. 'He's different now. I thought when I saw him again I'd feel the same, but . . . I don't know if it's me or him that has changed.' She looked at Stacie challengingly. 'Is he your lover?'

Stacie stiffened, flushing hotly, her hands tightening around her knees. 'If you mean have I been to bed with him—no, I have not!' It was the sober truth, but she knew she was being evasive; Marianne hadn't asked her the one question Stacie wouldn't have known how to answer. If Marianne had asked her if she was in love with Nicholas, her response would have been very different, but as it was she was able to speak clearly and fiercely, and Marianne looked stricken.

'Oh, I am sorry—that was unforgivable! I had no right . . . I shouldn't have listened to Tony, I might have known he was putting two and two together and making five, but I thought if Nicholas had fallen in love with someone else it would explain why he seemed so changed.' She brushed her straight silky blonde hair back from her face, her hands trembling. 'I'm just no good at all this . . . I hate scenes and arguments, that's why I haven't talked to Nicholas about the future. I couldn't bear it if he started to get angry, when he's angry he's terrifying.'

'I know,' Stacie said drily, then they both jumped as the door opened and someone looked at them. It wasn't Nicholas, though—it was his mother and she seemed angry.

'What happened to Tony's face?' she demanded of them both. 'He says he walked into a door, but I don't believe it.'

Neither of them said anything, and after a pause she said discontentedly: 'Well, the lunch is almost ready, I gather. Are you staying, Miss Murray?' and she looked with pointed lack of invitation at her watch. 'Or must you be on your way?'

'She's staying,' Nicholas said behind her, and Mrs Kinsella started, looking round.

'Nicholas! Tony isn't coming down to lunch, he's hurt his mouth and says he can't eat. He *says* he walked into a door.'

'Perhaps that will teach him to watch his step,' Nicholas drawled shamelessly, and his mother stared at him with suspicion.

Stacie got up and moved towards the door. 'I think I'll go and wash before lunch,' she said as she came face to face with Nicholas.

He stepped aside and she walked past without meeting his eye. She went upstairs into her room and looked at herself grimly in the dressing-table mirror. The situation in this family was too tangled to be comfortable; she didn't look forward to eating a meal with them all, even if Tony stayed sulking in his room. She didn't know whether to be sorry for Marianne or irritated with her, and she wasn't wild about Mrs Kinsella, either. She brushed her hair slowly, her face uneasy, then went into the bathroom to wash her face and hands before renewing her make-up. She could do with some clean clothes, perhaps Marianne could lend her something loose that might fit. They were not the same size, unfortunately, but they might find something.

She was drying her face when she heard a movement in her room and quickly opened the bathroom door to look out. Nicholas eyed her derisively as she flushed in anger.

'What are you doing in here?' she demanded.

'I wanted a private word with you before lunch.'

'How soon can I leave? Surely Nwanda's back in his own country by now?'

'He hasn't made the announcement yet, though.'

'What if he doesn't make it for days? You can't keep me here much longer—I want to get home for Christmas. You must let me leave tonight.'

His mouth hardened. 'I can't trust you not to break the story. You'll stay here until I say you can go.'

Stacie said bitingly: 'The longer I stay here the more trouble I'll make for you!'

He moved so abruptly that she was too late to get away from him, his hands bit into her shoulders and shook her violently. 'You've already done enough damage! If you're wise you'll stop while you're still in one piece—you're making me very angry, I warn you.'

Stacie lifted her head defiantly, green eyes flashing. 'You don't scare me, Mr Kinsella, and if you're sick of having me around the remedy is in your own hands, let me go.'

His eyes hardened further to dark points of steel that pierced her and made her shiver. 'I've no intention of letting you go,' and the words had a double meaning as his fingers tightened on her flesh, sinking into them so that the pressure made her wince. Their eyes warred bitterly, but all the time she felt his hands pulling her close, fraction by fraction, her feet obstinately rooted to the floor and refusing to shift, but her traitorous body arching obediently towards his and her pulses beginning to clamour for the contact he was urging.

'I insist . . .' she began, and Nicholas laughed harshly.

'You insist?' he mocked—and then her stammered protest was silenced under the ruthless heat of a kiss which made her nerves leap hectically in a pleasure she wished she could deny. His hands slid down her arms and closed around her, their bodies melting into each other, contours meeting and fitting as though they had been made to be one. She tried to drag her dissolving mind back to sanity, tried to remember how she hated and despised him for making love to one girl while he cold bloodedly intended to marry another. Her own senses defeated her, drowning her in a swirl of colour and sound and sweetness that made her weak. She forgot everything but the intensity of physical sensation, the magnet of his body holding her, controlling her against her will and all common sense.

It was a long time before Nicholas Kinsella lifted his head and as their mouths parted Stacie leant on him, shuddering. She was dazed with passion, incredulous at the force of her own reactions to him. It was all too sudden, too fast, too uncontrollable. It terrified her.

'You'll do as I tell you,' Nicholas ordered, and his cool voice was like the splash of icy water on her hot flesh. She took a sharp breath, looking at him with bitter hurt and anger. Had that long kiss meant nothing to him? Had he been using her own body against her?

'You bastard!' she whispered, her lips shaking. 'Don't give me orders! I'm not going to stay here . . .'

'Aren't you?' he mocked, and her flush was hectic at the look in those grey eyes.

'Men like you make me sick! You think you only have to snap your fingers and everyone will jump, don't you? Maybe nobody ever said no to you before—but I'm saying it now. I'm getting out of here, and nothing you can do will make me stay!'

He lifted one brow in cynical amusement. 'Nothing?' he drawled, and Stacie felt his hand slide up over her breast in a soft caress. Her whole body felt that seductive touch and that made her so angry that she totally lost her temper.

Wrenching away, she hit him across the face, so hard it made a noise like a pistol shot. Nicholas froze, the intake of his breath fierce, while Stacie stared at him, appalled by what she had done. He had gone white with rage and the mark of her fingers showed up lividly on his cheek. She backed, trembling, sure that he was going to hit her back, but instead his arm shot out and she winced as his fingers grabbed her hair. He jerked her head back, his arm clamping round her. Stacie was helpless against his strength; he forced her backwards and his lips bruised her mouth in a long, painful possession that was worse than any blow; the kiss hurt and was intended to hurt, neither of them got any pleasure from it.

He released her and as she shakily touched her swollen lip watched her with brooding eyes. 'Don't hit me again,' he said curtly. 'Next time I might hit you back.'

'I'd prefer it!' Stacie muttered, still tasting her own blood. 'You're an animal!'

'Aren't we all?' he retorted without any visible sign of regret. 'Now, what did Tony say to you this morning? If you print any of it . . .'

'Just get out of here and leave me alone,' gritted Stacie, her green eyes dark with contempt. 'You don't need to repeat the warning. Is it my fault if your brother chooses to confide in me? I didn't set out to pump him, you know—he came out to find me, I didn't go looking for him. Your brother and I have something in common, and I'm sorry for him!'

He frowned angrily. 'What do you have in common?'

She looked at him directly, coldly. 'We both hate the sight of you.' She turned away before he could answer that. 'Your mother will be wondering what's keeping you, hadn't you better go down to lunch?'

'If you're ready . . .' he said, and she shook her head.

'I haven't put on my make-up yet. I won't be long.'

Nicholas hesitated. 'Don't be,' he said at last, moving to the door. 'And don't let me see you with Tony again.'

When he had gone Stacie sat down on the bed, her legs buckling, and she was afraid she might keel over if she didn't sit down soon. Her mouth throbbed and burnt, there might be a bruise there tomorrow, and if his mother asked her how she got it she would tell her the truth, whatever the consequences from Nicholas. She tentatively touched her lip, shivering at the recollection of that brutal kiss. He had meant to hurt her, damn him. He was a swine. Why did she always have to fall for men like that? Or was it only swine that she found irresistible?

Until she found herself telling Marianne about it, she had forgotten the only other time she had been in this sort of emotional turmoil. It had been so long ago and she had been so young and it had been an indelible lesson, one she had taken years to get over, but the pain had been so bad that she had willed herself almost desperately to forget him, the selfish egoist who had given her three months of wild happiness and unbearable misery. She had even forgotten his name, his face, forced them out of her conscious mind and kept them out until today when she began to talk to Marianne about it spontaneously, taking herself by surprise. Back it had all come in one tidal surge—from forgetting entirely she had instantly remembered everything, every tiny detail.

The years between had taken the sting out of the memory, though. She could smile wryly at her earlier self: naïve and eager and hopelessly vulnerable. She had thought him so macho, so excitingly male, and he had been a vain, sadistic devil who got a thrill from exploiting the emotions of girls too young to see him as he really was. He had been part of her education: not the formal side when you sat in a desk and made notes as the teacher droned away, but the learning process you began when you left school and tried to pick up adult ways of thinking without anyone deliberately teaching you. Nobody teaches you how to cope with hurt and rejection, anxiety and uncertainty about yourself. Those lessons you learn alone, painfully, by experience, and the scars inflicted can sometimes last you all your life, however carefully you hide them. They can dictate how you will react in other situations, towards other people, they can be dangerous because you can make mistakes through being too wary of taking risks. Risk-taking is part of living, avoiding it can be disastrous too.

Stacie grimaced at her reflection as she did her make-up. Why wasn't it easier to cope with living? Who drew up the game rules and why did they put in so many penalties for mistakes?

As she outlined her mouth with glossy pink she felt her lip throbbing; it was puffy and misshapen. Tomorrow it would be bruised visibly, a dark blue shadow on her flesh. What should she say to Mrs Kinsella? She stifled a giggle. 'I walked into the same door as Tony?' She could imagine Mrs Kinsella's face. What would the other woman reply? 'What sort of door, pray?' she might ask in a haughty voice, and Stacie would tell her; 'Thick and wooden,' and look at Nicholas to make sure he got the point. At times she thought she caught a fleeting humour in his eyes, sometimes he smiled at her as though he enjoyed their little spats, at others he reverted to his King Kong status and began roaring and beating his chest in rage. That was when Stacie got worried and annoyed. She didn't want to find herself being carried off, tiny and wriggling, in his enormous paw.

She looked at her watch, sighing. She might as well go down before he came to look for her. If she had to be in his company she preferred it to be among other people; it was safer.

She was halfway down the stairs when she noticed that the front door was open and the winter wind blowing like an arctic gale through the house. Before she had got to the bottom step she heard Tony's voice raised angrily outside.

'I'm going for a drive to get some fresh air—I'm stifling in that house!'

'Does Mr Kinsella know?' That was Roughton, doggedly obstinate, and Tony reacted to his tone like hot fat when water splashes into it.

'What the hell do you mean by talking to me like that? Who do you think you are?'

'I'm only following orders, sir,' Roughton said,

unworried by his rage. 'Your brother said nobody was to leave the grounds without his permission.'

'Damn him to hell—and you too!' Tony's voice was suddenly nearer, he was walking back into the house. Stacie hurriedly limped behind the open door, out of sight, not wishing to get involved.

'Hey, you!' Tony snarled a few feet away, just on the other side of the door, and for a second Stacie thought he had seen her, then she realised that he was still talking to Roughton.

'Come with me. You want to hear my brother give me permission to leave the grounds? You're going to. And you're going to hear me telling him what I think of your damned insolence too!'

Roughton didn't answer, but Stacie heard his heavy footsteps and shrank further behind the open door, hoping neither of them would look round and see her. They walked past down the hall and she watched their backs. Her mind was suddenly hyper-active with a new idea. Tony vanished into the dining-room and Roughton moved out of sight, too. Stacie tentatively edged out from behind the front door and looked through it.

A car was parked right outside; black and gleaming. Stacie shot a quick glance down the hall. There was still no sign of Tony or Roughton. If she was quick she could get out of the house and into the back of the car before they came back. It was a risk; Nicholas might very well refuse to let his brother go and then she might be discovered and brought back into the house to face Nicholas's anger, but Stacie was in a mood to take risks.

She hurried out, hoping no other member of the security force guarding the house would see her. She hadn't seen any of the men with their dogs all morning, perhaps they were only on watch at night. During daylight hours it was probably sufficient to have Roughton around to keep an eye on the grounds.

Opening the back door of the car, she got inside, closing it as quietly as she could. She crouched down between the seats, keeping her head low. To her relief the car had windows which were placed quite high, the glass smoky, so that it wasn't easy to see inside the vehicle. No doubt they were bullet-proof.

It seemed an eternity as she waited heart beating fiercely, listening for the sound of someone coming. She felt sweat trickling down inside her clothes, making them stick to her flesh. It was stupid to be so scared—what could they do to her? But she knew what it was that was frightening her: it was the thought of being discovered and ignominiously dragged in front of Nicholas. He would be very angry, and Stacie's nerves leapt at the prospect of facing that rage.

Suddenly she heard voices. 'Get those gates open!' That was Tony, sounding triumphant. 'And I mean now!'

His footsteps grated on gravel as he walked round the car. Stacie crouched lower, tensely waiting. She heard the car door open and the springs give as Tony got into the driver's seat.

Please don't let Roughton come down and look into the car, Stacie prayed, eyes squeezed shut. She heard the engine flare into life, roar, then the car shot forward at tremendous speed and accelerated. Stacie didn't dare to move yet, she had to be certain they had gone through those gates before she let Tony know she was in the car. Even now they might be stopped. If Nicholas grew suspicious of her long absence and went upstairs to find out why she hadn't appeared for lunch he would find the room empty and come down at a run to order Roughton not to open the gates.

They could only be operated from the house, Tony would have to go back if they didn't open, and then they would look in the car and find her and pull her out to confront Nicholas.

She felt the car slowing and her pulse raced violently. Had they realised she had gone? Were the gates still shut?

The car rolled forward, it didn't stop, she felt Tony shift in his seat and then the car swung to the right and the speed went up again as he drove onwards, and she knew they were on the open road which passed the walls of the house. She heard another car pass them, going in the opposite direction. Tony seemed to be doing around eighty miles an hour, although the car purred smoothly without effort. Stacie tentatively raised her head, uncoiling after it. She took a quick look through the smoky windows to check that she wasn't mistaken and saw a cottage flash by, its front window gleaming with Christmas lights. They were out of the grounds and travelling very fast indeed.

'What the . . .' Tony suddenly noticed her, exclaiming; the shock made his hand slip on the wheel, and the car went out of control, skidding on the icy road with a screech of tyres. Swearing under his breath, Tony gripped the wheel with both hands, wrenching it to the left as he righted the zigzagging course. For a minute he was forced to concentrate on his driving and Stacie sat down on the back seat, stretching her cramped legs and massaging them to make the blood circulate more freely.

'Where did you spring from?' asked Tony when he could safely spare some attention for her, looking at her over his shoulder. 'What the hell are you doing in my car?'

'Keep your eyes on the road—there's black ice all over the place and I don't want to be an accident statistic.'

'Back seat driver,' he said truculently, but obediently turned to look back at the road. He glanced up at his mirror to watch her reflection. 'What's going on? When did you get into the car?'

'While you and Roughton were talking to your brother,' Stacie admitted with triumph.

'Nicholas doesn't know . . .'

'Would I go through contortions like that if he did?' she asked drily, and Tony's brows knit thoughtfully.

'You mean it was the truth? What you said about Nicholas refusing to let you leave?'

'It was the absolute truth,' Stacie assured him, looking at the name of the village through which they were driving at a pace which made some women standing outside the one small shop turn and stare in disbelief. 'Can you take the next turning on the left here?'

Tony slowed as he approached the crossroads outside the village and took the left hand turn without querying her request. On either side of them bare, skeletal trees rattled in the winter wind; the lane was deeply sunken and wound ahead through flat fields whose recently ploughed earth showed brown and ridged between gaps in the tangled hedge.

'Where are we going?' asked Tony.

'You're taking me home,' Stacie said cheerfully. She was euphoric at having escaped, soon she would be with Helen and Roland and the children just in time for Christmas. She would ring William at once and give him the story, she decided; it might be safest. Once she had done that there would be no point in Nicholas trying to interfere with her again.

'Nicholas will soon realise you've gone,' Tony said slowly. He was a very slow thinker, Stacie decided, he was just working things out now and looking worried. 'He'll realise you must have gone with me. The only way you could have got out was in my car.'

'So what? He can't do anything to me now . . .' She was too elated to care about anything.

'He can to me,' said Tony in trepidation, the car slowing.

'Hey, don't slow down!' Stacie burst out, nervously peering over her shoulder at the road behind them. 'He may be following us. We don't want him to catch us up, do we?'

'Not so much of the we!' Tony told her, down to a snail's crawl. The speedometer registered ten miles and Stacie was alarmed. 'Don't count me in on whatever you're up to,' he added heartlessly. 'You haven't been telling me everything, have you? There's a lot more behind this than I realised. Why wouldn't Nicholas let you leave? Why are you so desperate to get away?'

'Oh, why can't you ask him all about it later?' Stacie seethed. 'Just take me home, Tony, be a darling . . .'

'Don't try to sweet-talk me! If you want me to help you, you'll tell me what's going on!'

'I want to spend Christmas with my family, not with your damned brother,' Stacie explained, leaning forward to draw level with his profile. Tony slid a look sideways at her, one eye on the road. 'Oh, Tony, you can't be so mean as to refuse to help me!'

'I'm not so sure I want you to go,' Tony said grudgingly. 'If you're not there Nicholas may turn his attention back to Marianne, and I don't want that.'

Stacie could have hit him, she had to hold on to her temper to stop herself from insulting him.

'Oh, please, Tony!' she pleaded instead, putting a supplicant hand on his arm, and he looked right round into her wide green eyes. Stacie filled them with every ounce of persuasion she could muster. 'Please!' she begged.

'He'll kill me,' Tony told her. 'You know that, don't you? He'll be beside himself with rage!'

Stacie heard the half-reluctant glee in his voice at that prospect and said at once: 'He'll be livid! But he won't be able to do a thing about it.'

'Oh, won't he?' Tony said more gloomily. 'You don't know him. I wouldn't bet on it.'

'All right,' said Stacie, throwing caution to the winds. 'It's a risk. He may go berserk. He may tear up the floorboards and batter you senseless with them. He may eat nails and spit them at you. But haven't you any gambler's instincts? Aren't you going to risk it just for the kick of seeing his face when he realises he's too late to do anything to get me back?'

Tony visibly swayed, torn this way and that between conflicting impulses all of which had their basis in his alarm and resentment towards his brother.

'No,' he said. 'I can't—I think I'd better drive straight back to the house before he catches up with us and beats the hell out of me.'

'You can't do that to me, Tony!' Stacie protested. 'Don't be such a rat!' She grabbed at the door handle. 'Well, I'll walk if I have to . . .' They were going so slowly that it wasn't dangerous to jump out, she would land on the grass by the roadside and she might get a few bumps and bruises but nothing serious.

Tony's hand shot out and grabbed her wrist. 'Okay, okay—you win! I don't want you breaking your other ankle.'

'You'll take me home?' she asked, still poised to jump once she had opened the door.

'Scout's honour,' he said.

'Were you a scout?' Stacie asked suspiciously, and he grinned.

'Not on your life, but I won't break my word, don't worry. I'll take you home,' and the car accelerated again along the road leading to her sister's home.

'Stop before we get there,' she said cautiously. 'I know a back way I can take—if Nicholas has got here first he'll be parked round the front. Drop me and I'll make my own way after that.'

'I wish I knew what this was all about,' Tony complained. 'You might give me a little more information—I feel I have that much owed to me.'

'You'll be better off knowing nothing,' she assured him, and he looked even more alarmed and stopped badgering her, nodding. Stacie directed him until they were almost within sight of Helen's house and then told him to stop.

'This is where I get out.'

'Sure you'll be okay?' he queried with belated compunction as she opened the door.

'Certain.' Stacie looked both ways before she ducked out of sight between a double line of hazel trees climbing a low hill. She heard Tony drive away and looked back. The road was empty. It was a two-minute walk across the hill and the public footpath she was taking crossed the end of Helen's garden. The one worry Stacie had was that Nicholas had arrived and had had time to find out from Helen that there was another way to the house. Stacie wouldn't like to meet him out here where nobody would see them or hear her if she yelled for help.

She stopped in her tracks as she saw something moving among the bushes ahead of her. A second later she knew it was a man, and her nerves tensed as she tried to work out whether she could sneak past without him seeing her. Or had he seen her already? She couldn't see his face. It could be an innocent stranger— but on the other hand it could be Nicholas or Roughton.

She slipped from tree to tree, every sense alert. The other figure vanished suddenly. He was hiding, waiting for her. Stacie stopped dead, so jumpy she almost screamed as someone touched her on her shoulder.

CHAPTER SEVEN

'WHATEVER are you doing, creeping about like that?' asked Roland's voice, 'I heard rustling and panting and I thought it was a fox, so I sneaked round a bush to watch it and it turned out to be you ... are you all right, Stacie? Whatever's the matter?'

She faced him, a hand to her heart, which was going like an express train, and gave him a sarcastic smile.

'You scared the living daylights out of me, that's what's the matter—imagine coming up behind me and putting your hand on my shoulder without warning!'

'Your nerves are bad,' he said, eyeing her professionally. 'Too many late nights. That job of yours can't help much, either, far too much tension involved. Whenever I feel work is getting on top of me I come up here where it's quiet and watch the birds.' He indicated the binoculars which hung around his neck. 'That slows the pulse down, you should try it.'

'You watch the birds?' Stacie queried. 'And it slows your pulse down? Have you told Helen this interesting theory?'

Roland laughed after a minute's careful consideration of that. 'You've got a disgusting mind! You know I meant the feathered variety. I'm a happily married man, remember—Helen tells me so a dozen times a day. Did she send you up here to look for me? She wanted me to get out from under her feet just now, said I was in her way. You got your job finished earlier than they expected, didn't you?'

Stacie stiffened. 'Job? What are you talking about?'

Her fierce tone made Roland take a backward step, his face alarmed. 'I don't know,' he placated. 'Whatever you went to do, I suppose. Don't worry, they told us it was confidential and you couldn't talk about it. They explained that . . .'

'Who did? Who? Who?' Stacie burst out like a stuttering owl, and Roland looked at her as though he was beginning to fear for her sanity.

'Whoever rang—I didn't talk to them, I was in the surgery. Helen did, you must ask her. Stacie, your nerves are far too edgy, you need a long break. If you push yourself too hard . . .'

Stacie didn't wait to hear the rest of that warning; she was hurrying away down the slope towards his house as fast as her sprained ankle would allow. She opened the wicker gate that led into his garden, hearing Roland coming down the hill more slowly. The garden was locked in the grip of winter; the trees stripped and bare, creaking in the wind, and the grass stiff with frost from the night before, the dull grey light from the sunless sky making the whole scene mournful. Stacie shivered briefly, but she was racing against time and Nicholas Kinsella; she had to get to a phone before he caught up with her. Her restless agitation left no room for winter's depression.

She opened the kitchen door and found the room full of delicious odours, children, Helen and a male figure which made Stacie do a double-take with nervous alarm before she recognised it and sagged in relief.

'William!'

For a minute the kitchen erupted with noise as everyone tried to talk at once, then Helen shouted: 'Shut up, all of you!' at the children, who subsided, and Stacie hugged William, who looked self-conscious under Helen's approving smile but kissed Stacie warmly all the same. 'When did you get here?' asked Stacie when he had stopped.

'I only just got here myself,' he explained. 'Where have you been? I've been worried about you. I rang this morning and when your sister said you'd been sent off on a confidential job I rang the paper to find out what was up, and the Picture Desk denied knowing anything about it. I thought at first that it was typical, one hand doesn't know what the other hand's doing . . . I got tough and said; check, will you? Just check it out with everyone who was on last night! I rang back half an hour later and they still said you hadn't been sent on a job and I could tell they were laughing at me, they thought you'd stood me up and used the paper as an excuse.' He grinned at her. 'I admit I wondered, myself . . . but then I remembered Kinsella and I decided to come down and see if I could pick up a trail.' He paused and eyed her enquiringly. 'So, what happened?'

Helen was staring at her, eagle-eyed as ever. 'Stacie! What have you done to your foot?'

'Oh, it's nothing—just a sprain,' she dismissed. 'William, I've got the story of a lifetime for you, a real scoop, this will make sure you get that job . . .'

His eyes lit up. 'I knew it! I had one of those hunches, if I was a woman I'd call it female intuition . . .'

'How did you sprain your foot?' Helen insisted as Roland came through the door in his stockinged feet having left his muddy boots outside, and Roland looked sharply at Stacie.

'Good lord, I didn't even notice,' he said ruefully. 'I'm a great diagnostician, aren't I? Is it painful?'

She grinned at him. 'You were so busy worrying about my mental state that you didn't have time to notice anything else!'

'Don't rub it in,' he pleaded. 'You'd better let me take a look at it now.'

'Later,' said Stacie. 'I've got to talk to William alone first. Can we use your office for a little while?'

'Yes, so long as you promise not to touch anything. Those papers on my desk may look untidy, but they're arranged exactly the way I want them and if you move them I may never find some of them again.'

'I promise,' said Stacie.

'Are we allowed to ask what's going on in our own house?' demanded Helen. 'You still haven't told us where you were all night—and how did you sprain your ankle? What have you been up to, Stacie? I know that look, I don't like it when you look like that, it always means trouble. You've never been a peaceful person, you don't seem happy unless you're whistling up a whirlwind . . .'

Stacie looked at the kitchen clock, going pale. 'There isn't time to tell you now. I must talk to William before he gets here.'

'He? Who?' asked Helen, ears pricking at this mention of a man. 'Stacie, what have you been doing?'

Stacie was already pulling William out of the room and didn't bother to answer. A whirlwind was precisely what would hit them when Nicholas Kinsella arrived, but it would be time enough to warn Helen about him when he showed up. Stacie had little doubt he would come; she knew him too well by now, he wouldn't give up that easily, although there was nothing he could do to stop the story once she had given it to William.

As she led him into Roland's office William stared at her, his face thoughtful.

'I'd like to know who "he" is, too,' he said mildly. 'Would he be the guy who rang your sister and told her you'd gone on a job?'

'Probably,' said Stacie, her teeth meeting as she thought about that. Yes, Nicholas had probably made that call himself—cool as a cucumber, lying his head off and doing it so smoothly that he didn't arouse Helen's suspicions for an instant. Stacie knew her sister. Helen wasn't that easy to fool and she would have been dying of curiosity. Nicholas must have used every ounce of charm and authority to stop her asking questions.

'Your sister was amazed when I told her the paper didn't know where you were—it never entered her head for a minute that the guy who rang was lying.'

Stacie laughed angrily. 'Oh, I'm sure he was very convincing,' she said with a force that made William's eyes widen. She looked away from the question in his face and limped towards the desk. Her foot ached and throbbed so much now that she felt slightly sick, although the tremors in her stomach could be caused by the tension of the past twenty-four hours. She sat down with a long sigh and William perched on the desk beside her, trying to see her face, which she nervously kept turned away.

'Well? So where have you been all night?' asked William, and she looked round at him then, knowing she was going to startle him.

'With Nicholas Kinsella,' she said triumphantly, and saw William's face freeze in shock.

'What?' he almost shouted, and she was puzzled by the hardness of his voice and the blankness of his eyes, until it suddenly dawned on her what he thought, how he had interpreted what she had said. It would have been funny if it hadn't been so nearly true, and her face ran with colour as she hurriedly shook her head.

'No, William, not in bed . . .' It might well have been, of course, but she saw no reason to tell him that. The personal side of what had happened last night was not part of the story she wanted to see in print; she wasn't going to confess to anyone that she found Nicholas Kinsella wildly attractive or that if it hadn't been for the intervention of fate she might have let him make love to her. She didn't even want to remember it, and she would take good care that she stayed out of his way in future. He was a ruthless egotist who would only hurt any woman stupid enough to love him. She had known him such a short time, it seemed incredible how few hours she had spent with him; yet he had already overturned her whole world and she would never think or feel in quite the same way after knowing him. A man who can make that much of an impact so quickly was a man to steer clear of ever after.

William relaxed slightly, shrugging off his brief alarm
and half-smiling. 'Well, I knew you couldn't mean *that*,
of course,' he said, to cover his own momentary
dismay. William had his own brand of egoism, every
man does; he leaned forward to kiss her and on a reflex
she shifted so that his lips only brushed her cheek. She
didn't quite know why she didn't want to meet his
mouth, but she was reluctant to do it at that moment.
Perhaps she felt guilty because she was lying to him, in
spirit if not in fact. If she was strictly honest with him
she would have to say: well, I nearly did sleep with him,
I wanted to, I wouldn't have stopped him. On the other
hand she wasn't sure what she would have done if his
family hadn't arrived just then. That moment had been
one of those paths down which one had not gone; with
hindsight how could one be certain of anything?

'You're not that sort of girl, I wouldn't love you if
you were,' he said, and sounded so self-satisfied that she
frowned. What sort of girl did he think it took to find
Nicholas Kinsella irresistible?

'So what is the story?' William asked when she was
silent, and she pulled herself together and began to tell
him from the beginning, and he listened, hypnotised,
especially when she mentioned Saul Nwanda.

'Are you sure it was him?' he interrupted, and she
nodded impatiently.

'Of course I'm sure.'

'You got pictures of them both?' William was excited,
he couldn't keep still; he slid off the desk and began
pacing about as though he was writing the story in his
head already.

Stacie grimaced. 'I got them—but they've been
destroyed, I'm afraid. Nicholas Kinsella took the film
out of my camera.'

He stared at her and sat down again, pulling a
notebook out of his pocket. 'I'd better get this down, I
might forget some of it.' He made some hurried

squiggles in what passed for shorthand, then looked up.
'Go on . . .'

'Then someone started shooting at me,' Stacie said,
and his mouth dropped open.

'You're kidding!'

'Do I look as though I was kidding?' She
remembered her own incredulity when the bullet hit the
tree beside her and saw the same feeling mirrored in
William's brown eyes.

'Good lord,' he muttered, scribbling, then looked up
with concern. 'Hey, is that how you hurt your foot? Did
they hit you?'

'No, I did that when I fell off the tree; they wouldn't
have caught me otherwise. I'd have been in my car and
away before they got out of the gates if I hadn't been
limping.' She went on with her story and William wrote
fast, muttering his amazement under his breath from
time to time but not interrupting again in his eagerness
to get the story down on paper.

She was almost hoarse by the time she got to the end,
and when she stopped talking William looked up,
absently massaging his right hand as if he had cramp
from writing so much so fast. His eyes were almost
feverish with excitement.

'What a story! You didn't find out anything about
these talks with Nwanda? No idea what it was about?'

'Some sort of massive loan, I think, but Nicholas
Kinsella was far too cagey to let anything like that slip
out.'

William glanced through his notes, frowning. 'I
wonder how much of this the lawyers will let us use?
Kinsella's an influential guy. He'll bring his own
lawyers down on us like a ton of bricks if he can—and
he may use the Home Office to stop us.'

'The Home Office?'

'Come on, Stacie—they must have known what was
going on!—Nwanda couldn't have got into the country

without the government knowing he was here—and
why! Before we print one word, you can bet your life
that the lawyers will insist on getting Home Office
clearance.'

Stacie's face clouded. 'I hadn't worked that out.'
Nicholas hadn't told her that the British Government
knew what was happening, but he had been oddly sure
of himself when she threatened him with the police. He
had laughed off her threats.

'I'll knock this into shape and phone it through,' said
William. 'Can I use the phone in here?'

'Of course,' she said, barely listening because she was
wondering why Nicholas hadn't yet shown up; she had
been so sure he would follow her, and she felt aggrieved
because he hadn't. It was inexplicable how oddly
certain she was about the way his mind worked—she
felt she could anticipate his every mood, pick up his
thoughts as if she were telepathic. She didn't know him,
of course, it was all illusory; he was a separate and alien
mind, an unknown country—yet she still had that
strange feeling one has arriving in a country never
visited before but to which one is deeply attracted on
sight, as if the new and strange was somehow familiar
and remembered. Stacie had felt sure Nicholas would
come bursting into her sister's house—and she had
planned exactly what she would say to him, she had
looked forward to it with impatient excitement. Even
quarrelling with Nicholas was an intense satisfaction; he
made her feel more alive than she had ever been before.

'Are you staying for Christmas?' she asked William.
'Helen would love to have you—she's very hospitable
and there's plenty of room.' She smiled and tried to
sound eager to have him there for Christmas, but when
he shook his head she was oddly relieved.

'I'd love to, but I must get back to London,' he told
her. 'I want to be on hand when the fighting starts. If
I'm not there to insist on the story going into the paper

the lawyers will have it all their own way.' William sounded exhilarated, he was a born journalist and the adrenalin of being on to a terrific story was making him high with excitement.

Stacie smiled understandingly, sympathetic. 'I'll let you get on with it, then,' she said, going out. She hadn't wanted William to stay, though, and that worried her the more she thought about it. Something essential had shifted in her feelings. She had never imagined she was in love with him, but she had thought it would happen one day. They had so much in common—a life style, a mental attitude, a mutual fascination for their work. They liked the same things; enjoyed the same jokes, wanted to see the same films and plays, read the same books and usually liked the same people. If they had been matched by computer they couldn't have been more compatible.

It was stupid, senseless, irrational—and yet she knew suddenly that she would never, now, fall in love with him. It wouldn't happen. Perhaps it never would have done, however long she had waited, even if she hadn't met Nicholas Kinsella.

It wasn't that she preferred Nicholas, or fancied herself in love with *him*; Stacie was too sensible to allow herself to go that fast. But Nicholas had shown her all too clearly that she hadn't understood the nature of the male–female relationship or what she herself wanted and needed from it. All these months she had been telling herself how nice William was—how much she was learning about him, how close they were, what fun they had together, what a marvellous couple they would make. And then when she met Nicholas Kinsella she had been like dry tinderwood struck by lightning. She had blazed up instantly without knowing or under- standing anything about him, only that when he touched her it made her go crazy.

She opened the kitchen door and Helen looked round

from the stove where she was making something that smelled delicious. She waved a wooden spoon at Stacie. 'Are you going to tell us what's going on or not?' she demanded aggressively.

Stacie bent her head and licked the spoon. 'Mmm . . . sensational! What is it?'

'Brandy butter sauce for the Christmas pudding. Don't change the subject. Where's William?'

Through the kitchen window Stacie saw Roland and the children in anoraks and wellies working in the garden. They looked ruddy and happy and were doing more laughing than working, although the sky had an even more leaden hue now and the wind had grown stronger and colder.

'He's on the phone to London, to the paper—it will be a long call, when he rings off I'll get the operator to tell me how much it cost and I'll pay Roland.'

'Don't be silly,' Helen said sharply, and at that second the door bell rang and Stacie jumped as if she had been shot.

'I knew it was too good to last,' said Helen, drying her hands, and taking the pan off the stove. 'I hope it isn't the start of an epidemic. We had rubella last Christmas, every child in the district seemed to get it—Roland hardly had time to show his face in the house, let alone enjoy his Christmas.'

'Don't answer it!' Stacie said frantically as her sister moved towards the door and Helen looked at her indulgently, laughing and shaking her head.

'Believe me, I wish I dared, but that's Roland's job and we're stuck with it. Mum always said I shouldn't marry a doctor.' She carried on remorselessly towards the door.

'Helen, don't open it!' Stacie almost shrieked, and Helen seemed startled.

'Why not?' she asked in sudden suspicion. 'Who do you think it is?'

Faced with her sister's curiosity, Stacie gave up, she gestured helplessly. 'Oh, go ahead, let him in . . .'

'Him?' Helen's ears pricked up at the pronoun, as always, and she looked at the closed door of Roland's office, with what she no doubt supposed to be enlightenment dawning on her face. 'Oh, I *see*—you don't want William to run into this other one? I must say, you're a dark horse, who is it? Do I know him?'

Stacie walked back into the kitchen with what she hoped was great dignity and sat down on the nearest chair. She told herself it was only because her ankle hurt; it wasn't because her legs had apparently turned to jelly at the prospect of facing Nicholas. She refused to listen to the sound of Helen opening the door, even when a blast of wintry air entered the house along with the deep, cool tones of Nicholas Kinsella's voice.

'Mrs Laxton?'

'Yes,' Helen said dazedly, and Stacie knew as if she was watching her face that her sister was staring at him with awed admiration. Helen had always been susceptible until she met Roland; she liked tall men with leanly modelled faces. She would be a pushover for Nicholas Kinsella.

'You're Stacie's sister, then! I've heard so much about you,' said Nicholas, turning on the charm, and Stacie burned with impotent fury as she heard that. She couldn't sit here and listen to him, she erupted into the hall.

'Liar!' she yelled, and Nicholas looked down the hall at her, his brows lifting.

Helen looked round at her in appalled reproof. 'Really, Stacie!'

Behind Nicholas lurked Roughton, shouldering his way into the house as if to come for Stacie. She pointed an aggressive finger at him. 'And you can get your gorilla out of here, too!' she screamed at Nicholas. 'Go on—tell him to leave, he isn't coming in here!'

Nicholas glanced at Roughton and nodded his head. 'You can wait in the car,' he said without inflection, and Roughton shambled out of the house, giving Stacie a reproachful look as he went. 'Calling me a gorilla— that's not nice, miss,' he said, his large body huddled against the cold wind as he met it.

'You've hurt his feelings,' Nicholas told her, and Stacie informed him through her teeth that she was glad.

'At least I didn't use a gun to do it,' she said, and Helen's jaw sagged.

Nicholas pointedly shivered, turning up the collar of his elegantly tailored camelhair coat. 'Could we have the door shut? This wind is like a knife.'

'Of course, do come in—I am sorry,' said Helen, in a hurry to ingratiate herself, and he closed the door and gave Helen another of his million-dollar smiles. She melted like a snowman in June.

'Come in here,' she said, opening the sitting-room door and ushering him into the room, while her eyes flew round it to make certain it was tidy. The children had left some comics on the couch, she hastily pushed them behind the cushions under a pretence of thumping the cushions back into shape. 'Do sit down, can I take your coat? The fire's very warm.'

Nicholas undid the buttons on his overcoat and slid out of it. Helen received it with reverence, her fingers automatically smoothing the expensive material.

'Would you like a drink? We have some whisky or . . .'

'I'd love a cup of tea,' said Nicholas, and then offered his hand. 'I haven't introduced myself—I'm your neighbour, a few fields off—Nicholas Kinsella.'

Helen had been smiling, but now her lips froze and a startled noise emerged. 'Nicho . . . oh!'

'We haven't met before, but I do know your husband, by name, at least. He's been over to visit us recently. I don't know what we would have done if there hadn't been such a good doctor right on the spot, my housekeeper was in great pain.'

Helen wasn't really listening to him, she was looking at Stacie in wild surmise and Stacie was trying not to notice her sister's stare. Nicholas sat down on the couch and held his hands out to the flames.

'Wonderful to see an old-fashioned log fire again,' he murmured. 'Oh, by the way, Stacie, I brought your car back, it's parked outside.' He looked at her sideways through his lashes and she felt herself smiling back at him, because although his remark had been casual his eyes were not, they talked to her so eloquently that her own eyes answered instinctively, although one part of her mind found it maddening that of all people in the world this one man should be able to get through to her without words. They had flung plenty of words at each other over the past two days, but they had never really needed them to communicate. Some spark seemed to leap between them when they met, a mutual recognition that they were two of a kind. Stacie had never had any trouble understanding him; she often wished she had, especially when she saw one particular look in his eyes and felt her body go weak with an answering feeling.

'Your car?' queried Helen, throwing Stacie a look which was sharp and far from sisterly.

'She left it at my house,' Nicholas explained drily, amused by Helen's blatant interest.

'She didn't tell us she knew you,' Helen said accusingly, still staring at Stacie.

'Didn't she?' Nicholas pretended amazement. 'Well, isn't she secretive?'

'I'll make some tea,' said Stacie, wanting to hit him.

'I'll do it,' Helen announced, and Stacie somehow got the feeling that Nicholas had forced the offer out of her by sheer strength of will. It was even more maddening to see him smile a second later and the way Helen melted on receiving it.

'I've heard so much about you all,' Nicholas murmured.

'She hasn't told us anything about *you*,' Helen informed him tartly, and he smiled again.

'Were you shy, Stacie?' Nicholas enquired in a tender voice, and Helen's eyes widened. *She* couldn't see the mockery in his eyes. Stacie could, and she bared her teeth at him, staying well out of the reach of his long arm.

'I'll get that tea, then,' Helen said regretfully, going out and closing the door behind her.

A silence fell, the only sound the flicker of the flames tonguing the chimney and the crackle of the log as it split wider. Stacie stared at the blue and orange of the flames as though hypnotised by them. All the physical sensations she had come to recognise whenever she was with Nicholas Kinsella were back—her mouth was dry, her pulses rapid, her skin burning, although she was shivering as if with a chill.

'If you've come to try to stop me giving the paper that story, you're too late,' she said huskily. 'They've already got it.'

'You move fast,' he said, almost absently, frowning.

'I learnt that from you, then,' she muttered, and he leaned back on the couch and tilted his head to smile at her. It was just a smile, she told herself angrily, it wasn't a world-shattering event! Why should it have such an inexplicable effect on her? What was there in a mere smile to make hearts miss a beat and ears become deafened by the sound of the blood racing round a body?

'So you did learn something from me,' he said softly. 'I learnt quite a bit from you, too. Isn't that strange? We seem to have had a surprising effect on each other.'

Her throat was rough, she swallowed with difficulty.

'What are you doing here?' He was turning that charm on her now and she couldn't take it. For some reason she couldn't define it was absolutely essential that she stay angry with him and he was deliberately making that very hard. When he smiled his eyes were brilliant, their light riveted her and made her head swim.

'I just told you,' he said blandly. 'I brought your car back, I thought you might need it.'

'Thank you,' she said without sincerity.

'And I wanted to make sure you had got back safely,' he went on. 'I gather Tony dropped you some way from the house. It must have been a difficult walk with a sprained ankle.'

'You've seen Tony?'

He nodded, and she could just imagine the interrogation which had taken place. Poor Tony! 'Is he on bread and water?' she asked bitingly, and Nicholas gave her a dry smile.

'Did the two of you cook it up beforehand?'

'No, I got in his car while he was talking to you. He had no idea I was hiding in the back. When I popped up later, he almost had a heart attack.'

'That fits what Tony told me—but then no doubt you would have concocted a nicely dovetailed story.' His eyes were sharp and sarcastic. 'But don't worry, I don't blame Tony. He hasn't got the brains to think up anything so simple and foolproof, and you're more than he can handle, he must have been putty in your hands.'

'You're too kind,' she said, shaking with a desire to hit him. 'And now you've found out that the story has already gone off to the paper, you can get out of here and take your tame gunman with you. I've seen enough of the Kinsella family to last me a lifetime!'

Nicholas eyed her with narrowed eyes. 'If you go on shrieking at me like that, your lifetime may be a short one.'

Stacie laughed scornfully, her head thrown back and

the firelight glimmering on her dark red hair. 'You don't scare me! You need a gun to make you impressive.'

'Do I now?' he asked, his grey eyes gleaming in a way she did not like, and his hand shot out and caught her wrist as she started to back, because she had lied: he did scare her, and he didn't need a gun to do it. He had weapons far more lethal and far more terrifying.

He jerked on her wrist and pulled her off balance, she fell, struggling, and suddenly he had both arms around her and she knew he was going to kiss her. His head came down and Stacie's pulses went wild, she trembled violently—but Nicholas's mouth didn't touch her lips. He looked down at her, her red hair spilled out over the silk cushion on which her head lay and she saw the dark pupils of his eyes enlarge and glow. She stared into them, hearing him breathing, hearing the fast irregular beating of his heart above her own, and lost all sense of time. The moment stretched endlessly, she had no awareness of herself, staring into his eyes she felt everything else fall away and become nothing.

And then Nicholas sat up, breathing thickly. 'I may not scare you, but you sure as hell scare me,' he muttered. 'I don't understand this. You've really got to me, right under my skin. What are we going to do about it?' And he turned his head to look at her and smile wryly. His hand brushed a fallen strand of hair back from her throat, his fingertips light and arousing.

'Go back to Marianne,' Stacie said huskily, shuddering. 'We're not going to do anything about it. You're going to marry her, aren't you? I don't want any part of the sort of affair you're talking about.'

He frowned, rubbing his eyes. 'It seemed like a good idea at the time, getting married to her. She's a lovely girl and my mother wanted it. I'd been thinking for a couple of years that I ought to get married and have children. I'll be forty before I know where I am; I never intended to wait to get married until I was that old. It just happened. At first I didn't want to be tied down and then I was always too busy; you can't get seriously involved with anyone if you're always moving from place to place. I was never anywhere long enough to get to know anyone that well. Now and then I'd meet a girl I liked a lot, I'd see her for a few weeks and then I'd have to be off to Japan or Australia and it might be a couple of months before I saw her again. Marianne was the only girl I went on seeing all the time. I've known her all her life. Last year I started thinking: well, why not? I knew I wasn't in love with her, but I'm very fond of her, I thought we could be happy enough, and anyway, after a few years of marriage it wouldn't matter. I've never noticed that that magic glow lasted. I've seen my friends fall in love and marry, sometimes they get divorced, sometimes they seem very happy—but whichever way, the glow fades and suddenly they're just fond of each other. Why not forget the falling in love bit? I thought. Just go straight on to . . .' He paused, shrugging wryly. 'It was a nice theory.'

Stacie had listened intently, hearing the flat note of total sincerity in his voice; what he was saying was no surprise to her, he was confirming what Tony had told her, what she had worked out for herself. Nicholas had proposed to Marianne because she was a suitable wife, not because he was in love with her. Stacie guessed that Marianne knew it, too; perhaps last summer Marianne had been in love with him, briefly, and blinded herself to his real reasons for proposing, but once he had gone away she had slowly begun to realise and understand the truth.

His grey eyes stared fixedly at the fire, he almost seemed to have forgotten her. 'And once I'd committed myself I got cold feet. I almost ran away from her, poor girl. I knew I'd made a stupid mistake, but I didn't know how to get out of it.'

Stacie felt a surge of anger, she sat up, too, flushed
and tense as she looked at that hard profile.

'Why are you telling *me* this? You should be talking
to Marianne, not me. Don't you think you've hurt her?
You ask her to marry you, then vanish leaving her
wondering whether . . .'

'Do you think I don't know that?' he interrupted
harshly. 'You don't have to tell me I'm a heel, I don't
need telling. I'm just trying to explain how I got myself
into that fix.'

'You're trying to make excuses for yourself,' Stacie
told him scornfully, and he looked round at her,
grimacing.

'You don't pull your punches, do you?' He stared at
her, his eyes searching her face, and Stacie instinctively
looked down to hide any trace of emotion. She felt like
someone facing an enemy whose sword point is hunting
for weak places in their armour. Nicholas wanted to be
her lover, he didn't need to tell her that—her blood
informed her even if her mind had been slow to admit
it. But a lover can be an enemy too. Sometimes love is
too dangerous, especially when it flares up instantly and
uncontrollably between people separated by everything
but that wild impulse. She and Nicholas came from
different worlds, they were alien to each other by birth,
circumstance, background and society. They had
nothing in common; he did not belong in her world, she
did not belong in his.

He slowly put his hand out to lift her chin, trying to
make her look at him; the silence ached between them
with everything she was feeling and thinking and could
not say.

'Stacie,' he whispered, and his voice was shaking; she
felt the hunger in it as though the fingers lightly holding
her chin transmitted his emotions through every pore. If
she were blind and he did not speak she would know
the touch of his hand, she thought, and was shaken to

the core as she realised she was too late to stop herself falling in love with him. She already had.

'Don't you know what's happened?' he said huskily. 'You do, don't you? If I'd realised . . . but I don't have second sight, I can't see the future. How could I know I was going to meet you? One day I was walking around doing business and going through my day as usual. It's all so routine, now, I thought I liked it like that— reading my morning paper over breakfast, going through the day's work and every day the same as the day before. I've got my life so well organised. Then you hit me and I lost control of myself and everything around me.'

Stacie felt sick, torn between her common sense and her own feelings. It wouldn't work, how could it? If she listened to him, she would just get hurt—because he had been right just now, this sudden crazy passion couldn't last, it never did, nothing so white-hot and immediate could last for long. And when it faded, what would they have? What did they have in common? How could she cope with his world? With the unbelievable wealth beyond anything she could even imagine, with the security men with their guns guarding you against the world and keeping you captive at the same time so that you couldn't even dare to go shopping alone. Nicholas Kinsella led a strange life; she barely knew him, but she could see that. He never went anywhere alone. Roughton—or someone like him—was always on his heels. How could she face his friends, who would sneer and despise her, the way Mrs Kinsella did? Mrs Kinsella certainly wouldn't welcome her. She would always be an outsider and an interloper; and gradually Nicholas would start to see her that way, too, when he realised she did not belong in his world. No, it wouldn't work, better to break it off now.

She pushed his hand away and got up, unsteadily. 'You'd better go,' she said as she fled towards the door.

'Stacie!'

He was right behind her as she wrenched the door handle, and then they both heard the rattle of cups as Helen pushed the tea trolley down the hall. Had she been waiting to hear movement before she brought the tea? Stacie wondered grimly. She pulled the door open and Helen halted, smiling quizzically.

'Sorry to take so long,' she said, looking past Stacie at Nicholas.

'I'm afraid Mr Kinsella has to go now, Helen,' said Stacie, and her sister's face fell.

'Oh, but I've got his tea here,' she protested, pushing the trolley forward insistently so that Stacie had to move out of the way or get run over. Nicholas strolled back to the couch and sat down.

'That cake looks delicious—did you make it yourself?' he asked Helen, who preened like a conceited bird, nodding.

The office door opened and William appeared, his hair standing on end as if he had been running his fingers through it in agitation. 'I got one of the deaf typists,' he burst out as he saw Stacie. 'Couldn't hear a word I said—I had to spell the whole damned thing to her, and it took hours! I've just been talking to Atkins, he's holding the whole front page until the lawyers have had a look at the copy.' He grinned, brushing his hair down. 'I'm his blue-eyed boy tonight, though. Gerry hasn't got a hope of getting that job now, darling.' He came and hugged her. 'Did I tell you in the last hour that I loved you?' He kissed her lingeringly. 'Well, I do. I love you like crazy!'

They were standing on the threshold of the sitting-room, the door ajar. Stacie was rigid and deeply flushed. As William let go of her she said huskily: 'Would you like some tea, darling? Helen just made it.'

'I'd love some, but I've got to be off—I'm going to burn up the roads between here and London to get

back before the conference passes judgment on my
story.' He paused and corrected himself, grinning
apologetically at her. 'Our story, Stacie, I'm not
forgetting you got it for me.' He looked through the
door, seeing Helen standing by the trolley, a cup in her
hand. ''Bye, Helen, lovely to see you and the kids, give
them my love. Next time Stacie comes down I'll come
too—have a great Christmas, all of you. I wish I was
staying, but maybe next year?'

'It's always nice to have you here, William,' Helen
said cheerfully. 'We're always telling Stacie to bring you
with her.'

William hadn't noticed Nicholas, who was sitting
down on the high-backed couch, only the top of his
black head visible.

''Bye,' he said, kissing Stacie again. 'Happy
Christmas, love. See you when you get back. We'll have
dinner somewhere ultra special.'

'I'll walk to your car,' said Stacie, following him. She
did not want to go back into the sitting-room and face
Nicholas just yet, she didn't know what he was
thinking, but even through the door she had picked up
vibrations from him that she had not liked.

Roughton was sitting inside a long black limousine
reading a newspaper folded into a neat square. He
looked up as she and William emerged and stared at
them all the way to William's car. William buttoned up
his coat, shivering.

'Looks like snow,' he said, glancing up at the sky.
The afternoon was falling towards night; the air was
thick with grey dusk and it was much colder.

William unlocked his car and Stacie reached up to
kiss him as he glanced down at her. 'Drive carefully,'
she said.

'I'll ring you on Christmas Day,' said William.
'Around lunchtime?' He got into his car and closed the
door. The engine started and he smiled up at her, then

drove away, while she stood watching him, her arms around her body as she huddled in the icy wind.

As she slowly turned away she saw Roughton getting out of his seat and stiffened, wondering if he meant to make trouble, but then she saw Nicholas coming out of the house. Roughton opened the back door of the car and stood to attention.

Stacie walked slowly, unwilling to meet Nicholas. He looked the way he had looked the first time she met him; hard, cold, inimical, those grey eyes piercing her without warmth.

He paused and surveyed her from head to foot. 'Goodbye, Miss Murray,' he said, and she couldn't even form a polite reply, her mouth seemed frozen.

He walked past and got into the car, and as Stacie reached the front door of the house she heard the car sweep purringly down the road. Helen was in the sitting-room gloomily looking at the practically untouched tea trolley. As Stacie joined her she looked up, scowling.

'He drank one cup of tea and went, and I took a lot of trouble with all this . . .'

Stacie sat down and took a plate and a slice of rich fruit cake. 'Never mind, I'll enjoy it.' Her hands were shaking and she felt Helen staring at them, so she held them out to the fire, saying hurriedly: 'It's freezing outside—I don't know how Roland and the children can stand it.'

'They're indoors now, in the kitchen having their own tea,' said Helen. 'I don't know why Mr Kinsella couldn't stay, he seemed to want some cake and then he didn't eat it.' She eyed Stacie teasingly. 'It was William, wasn't it? He didn't know about William. I hope you know what you're doing, keeping two of them on a string—no wonder you kept asking so many questions about him yesterday, why didn't you say you knew him that well? When did you meet him? I wish you weren't so secretive.'

'What did you tell him about William?' Stacie asked, forcing herself to swallow some of Helen's gorgeous cake. Her throat was so dry it was like eating sawdust, but Helen was offended enough by Nicholas's failure to eat the cake so Stacie went on eating.

'I didn't tell him anything,' Helen said indignantly. 'I'm not indiscreet, I could see from his face that he was angry, and when he got up and said he had to be going I tried to persuade him to stay and wait for you to come back.'

Nicholas wouldn't need to have anyone fill in the finer points of the picture; he would have worked it out for himself when he heard Stacie and William talking. Stacie didn't doubt his intelligence or his ability to put two and two together.

'This cake is fantastic,' she said, taking another slice and hoping she was going to be able to finish it. There was no reason why Helen shouldn't have a wonderful Christmas even if she herself was going to be as miserable as sin. 'Mmm . . . I shouldn't, but I'll start my diet again on Boxing Day,' she said.

She was relieved, she told herself firmly. William's appearance had meant that she didn't have to lie to Nicholas or argue with him; she had been saved from a painful decision and an even more painful discussion. Now she would never see him again, and that would hurt for a while, but in time she would forget him, although she didn't know how she was going to get through this Christmas and keep smiling whenever anyone looked at her. She would have to act like mad to make sure that none of them guessed how she really felt. It would be unbearable if anyone else knew about this sick, bitter misery.

CHAPTER EIGHT

WILLIAM rang during the middle of Christmas morning while the sitting-room was still awash with gaily coloured gift paper and discarded red ribbons and the family were sitting around the fire, the children drinking milk and the adults coffee, while they recovered from the hectic excitement of opening the presents. Nobody felt like answering the phone. Roland made a weary face. 'Let it ring,' he said because he had the day off and his partner was taking all the calls from patients. 'Just one day in the year let the phone stop working,' he added piously, looking upwards with his hands folded in prayer.

'It's probably William,' Stacie predicted, and all three children jumped up and ran to pick up the phone with Stacie on their heels.

'Hallo?' said Robin, snatching it up, then his mouth dropped open and he clamped the phone closer to his ear, listening, before holding it out to Stacie. 'He says it's Father Christmas!'

Stacie laughed, 'It's William, I thought it was.'

'He said his reindeer was stuck on the roof,' Robin told his parents, going back to drink his milk. 'He's silly.'

The twins settled down to watch Stacie, Ann had her thumb in her mouth and an air of female conspiracy about her. 'Hallo, William,' said Stacie, and Ann nodded to her, smiling, a perfect and comic mimicry of her mother which almost had Stacie in hysterics.

'Happy Christmas! I loved your present,' said Stacie. William had given her a book of hilarious misprints from newspapers and a bottle of her favourite perfume.

'Both of them—did you read the book before you wrapped it?'

'Why do you think I bought it?' William said shamelessly. 'Happy Christmas, Stacie, thanks for the sweater—it fits perfectly, in fact I'm wearing it because my flat's like the frozen North today.' He asked if they were having a good time and she described the children's faces as they opened their presents, and William laughed.

'Sounds fun.' He paused, then said: 'It didn't get in, you noticed—our story!'

'Yes, I saw that—the lawyers?' Stacie had got over her first rage about it.

'Uh-huh, by the time they had decided it could be used in a discreet, chewed-up form it was too late to get into any edition and they've decided to hold it over until after Christmas.'

'But the official news will have been released by then!'

'I know, but what could I do? I got back to town to find urgent conferences going on between the editor and the lawyers and there was an embargo on the copy. I gather Kinsella moved fast. Even before I'd filed my story he'd prodded some Home Office guy into getting on to the editor. He must have rung them the minute he realised you'd got away.'

'Yes,' said Stacie, her face grim, then she caught Ann's worried expression and winked at her. The little girl's face relaxed and she grinned back.

'We'll have a behind-the-scenes story that nobody else will have,' William comforted. 'Atkins apologised to me, said it was tough luck, but I could have my byline on the story when it did go in—and he hinted that I was front-runner for the job now.'

'That's wonderful, William, I am glad,' Stacie said, and her fervour was partly because she felt guilty about him. He rang off and she helped Helen to pick up all the wrapping paper and gift tags, her mind occupied with William. He didn't know that everything had suddenly changed between them—and she couldn't tell him, it wasn't possible. If they had been lovers she could have been frank and said: 'I'm sorry, it's over,' but they hadn't got that far, they had been well on the way to falling in love at one time, she had thought they would; it had been a shimmering possibility in the future, like a distant rainbow, but now it had vanished and she couldn't put that insubstantial change into words.

What could she say to him? 'I've realised I'll never fall in love with you.' What could William do but look amazed and offended and say: 'Who asked you to?'

Of course, she didn't have to stop dating him. She could just go on the same way, pretending nothing had changed, but that wouldn't be fair to William. It was one thing to date him and wait for love to happen and another to be certain it never would. If they had just been friends with no suggestion of anything more, that would be different, too—but they had both known it was more than that.

When they first started going out together they had been merely colleagues; William had got some free theatre tickets, complimentaries, and asked if she would like to see the play, and a week later they had met again at an office party. They had become a recognised, official pair almost without knowing it; but the sexual side of that relationship hadn't grown as fast. Stacie was reluctant to commit herself to an intimate affair; she had learnt to be wary, she was afraid of getting hurt, her earlier experience of intense emotion made her hold back. One of the reasons she liked William so much was that she felt certain he wouldn't hurt her, he was far too nice, but now she knew that that hadn't been what she felt at all—she had liked William because she knew he *couldn't* hurt, she would never feel as intensely for him as she knew she could feel. It hadn't been a conscious realisation; it had been instinctive, but meeting Nicholas had ripped the veil from her eyes and she saw now all too clearly how she had been protecting herself and using William to do it, as she had used all the men she had dated before him.

For years she had been refusing to get too involved, backing off from emotion and lying to herself like a trooper. It was so easy to deceive yourself; the unconscious co-operated without a qualm. What had William's motives been? she wondered suddenly. He hadn't seem to want to put any fire into their relationship, either; he had apparently been content with the way things were and maybe William had reasons of his own, of which she had guessed nothing, for keeping the temperature cool. They had agreed early on that there was no point in talking about the past, they hadn't swapped memories or made private confidences, but William was attractive and lively, there must have been other girls before her. He didn't have a strong sex drive, that much had been obvious, he had never seriously tried to get her into bed. He was even-tempered and careful; his own temperament had made it easier for her to go slow with him, and at the same time, she saw now, had meant that she would never lose her head over him or with him.

William was a good friend and she liked him a lot, but he didn't turn her on; she didn't want him as a lover, she never had.

'You're very quiet,' Helen commented as they served the Christmas dinner, working together without hassle in the kitchen while the children and Roland watched a film on television. 'I always feel uneasy when you're that quiet. I wish I knew what you were up to—you still haven't explained where you were the other night or how you met Nicholas Kinsella. You haven't told me anything much at all, come to that—why are you so sneaky?'

'I want to enjoy a quiet Christmas,' Stacie explained, draining the carrots. 'I don't want to talk about work.'

'Is Nicholas Kinsella work?' Helen demanded with what she imagined to be sarcasm, and Stacie firmly told her: 'Yes, that's what he is,' which left Helen in a state of speechless disbelief. Before she had recovered from that the twins rushed in, blowing squeakers and wearing funny hats, and by the time Helen had chased them out again she had forgotten all about Nicholas and was calling for Roland to get the children's hands washed in time for the meal.

It was a peaceful Christmas on the surface; the children were happy and Stacie spent most of the time in front of the television in loglike contentment, but all the time she was fighting not to think about Nicholas and telling herself that it had been a mere sexual infatuation, a sudden physical attraction that would soon be forgotten.

She was still telling herself that when she drove back to London on a grey December day. The snow which had threatened to descend on Christmas Eve had fallen briefly, a flurry of light melting flakes which did not hang around on the ground and was gone by morning. The temperature had risen slightly and the roads back to the capital were jammed with returning cars, some of which still had snow on their roofs. The snow had been heavier in the north and some parts of the country were still deep in snowdrifts.

The following day she went back to work, but William had three days off because he had had to work through Christmas, so he went to visit his parents, which gave Stacie a breathing-space in which to try to work out how she could break off their relationship, gently, without hurting his feelings or getting bogged down in a difficult discussion. She saw him briefly in the office, but there were others around, she was able to talk and smile quite naturally.

Everyone was teasing her about the story which had appeared in the first edition of the paper to come out after the Christmas break. It had been carefully worded; Nicholas's lawyers had put the fear of God and the libel laws into the newspaper, but the editorial staff knew all about Stacie's little escapade and pulled her leg unmercifully about Nicholas. 'What didn't you tell William?' one reporter whispered, grinning. 'Is Kinsella as good as they say? He doesn't usually have to use guns to persuade girls to come home with him.'

'You've got a despicable mind,' Stacie said haughtily, walking away, and the men all roared with laughter. Stacie hadn't been amused. It had been too close to the truth.

The other papers had only had the official announcement made by Nwanda himself in his own country, but they followed that with long stories about the threats made by Nwanda's rebel opposition who had fled the country or disappeared into the remote hills to gather support and fight another day. The vast loan made to him by Nicholas's bank would give Nwanda a chance to consolidate his victory, and the rebels made bitter accusations against Nicholas and the international financial world, hinting that Nicholas would regret his deal with Nwanda.

'Sounds like an assassination threat to me,' William remarked when Stacie saw him in the office. 'I wouldn't give much for Nwanda's chances of surviving long. He's sitting on top of a powder keg.'

'William!' yelled Atkins, and the men sitting around the office grinned at Stacie.

'Stop distracting the guy! That was His Master's Voice . . .'

She put her tongue out and left. She had hardly got back to her own office when William rang, cock-a-hoop, to tell her Atkins had given him three days off—a little prize for having got a scoop the other papers had

envied. 'I'm going to see my old mum and dad,' he told
her. 'Mum's got laryngitis; she gets something wrong
with her throat every winter. I'll ring you when I get
back.' Stacie tried not to sound relieved.

The following day was a Saturday; as she didn't have
to work Stacie stayed in bed until gone nine, had a
leisurely breakfast, did a little housework and shopped
for food in the modern shopping precinct a block away
from her tiny flat. Once she had finished all those
routine chores the day stretched emptily in front of her,
which left far too much space for Nicholas Kinsella to
invade. She did not want to think about him, so she
took a bus to Oxford Street, which was only ten
minutes away. The shops were already holding
midwinter sales and in spite of the grey weather Oxford
Street was crowded with bargain-hunters. The
Christmas decorations flapped disconsolately in the
wind, and the gaiety had drained out of the tinsel and
fairy lights still festooning shop windows; they looked
tawdry and depressing.

Stacie had decided she needed a new winter coat; the
long-range weather forecast was predicting heavy falls
of snow in January. She wandered from Oxford Circus
to Marble Arch but didn't see anything she fancied at a
price she could afford, so she turned back and went into
Selfridges to buy herself some tights and have a cup of
coffee before making her way home. The ground floor
was thronged with people. She pushed her way through
them and paused at the Givenchy counter to stare
enviously at the displayed perfume she couldn't buy
herself. Christmas had wiped out her current account
and she was feeling poor.

'Hi!' a friendly voice said beside her, and she turned,
startled by the American accent, to find Marianne
standing next to her.

'Oh,' Stacie said vaguely, then dragged a smile into
her face. 'Oh, hallo.'

'I thought it was you,' Marianne smiled back. 'Are you doing what I'm doing? Looking for bargains? Don't you love sales?'

'Yes,' Stacie agreed without adding that she couldn't afford to buy anything much more expensive than a pair of tights. That wouldn't apply to Marianne. She wouldn't have to wonder if she could afford a new winter coat; the one she was wearing must have cost the earth—peacock blue with a white fox fur collar which stood up like a ruff around her small face, framing it exquisitely, the coat was of vaguely Russian style; with a tight slender waist and full sweeping skirts which ended in a deep white fur hem. Marianne's blonde hair had been drawn back off her face, emphasising the sculptured delicacy of it, and swept up on top of her head in a chignon which was mostly hidden beneath a white fur hat.

'Expecting snow?' Stacie asked her drily, and Marianne laughed, a hand touching the hat.

'Isn't it cute? I just bought it, and the coat—at Harrods. It's snowing back home and once we get our snow it stays for weeks. Boston winters are no picnic.'

'Are you going home soon?' Stacie wanted her to say yes, she wanted her to say Nicholas was going, too. She wanted both of them out of the country, out of her life.

Marianne nodded. 'In a week or so, I guess. We're visiting friends of Mrs Kinsella's at the moment, I think she plans to stay for the New Year. We're playing it by ear.'

'Did you come up from Norfolk for the day?' asked Stacie, glacing around with a sudden apprehension that Nicholas might turn up at any second. She was still so surprised to see Marianne that it hadn't quite sunk in yet; she had felt safe in London, she hadn't expected any of the Kinsella party would turn up here.

'No, we're staying here,' said Marianne with a touch of impatience as though Stacie was being stupid. 'I told you, we're staying with some people—in Kensington, not far from Harrods. Norfolk is so cold at this time of year and Mrs Kinsella wanted to do some shopping in London.'

Stacie wasn't going to ask if Nicholas was with them. Instead she asked: 'Is Tony in London, too?' and Marianne looked at her strangely, frowning.

'Yes,' she said with obvious reluctance. 'He came with me in the taxi. We walked to Harrods first, but I didn't find the shoes I was looking for, so we jumped into a taxi and came here. Tony's somewhere around, he's looking at the records.'

'Did you have a good Christmas?' Stacie was struggling with herself; she badly wanted to know if Nicholas was in London, but she refused to ask, if Marianne mentioned him casually that wouldn't be *her* fault.

'It was fun,' Marianne said flatly. 'Did you?'

'Yes, thanks.' There was a silence and Stacie felt uncomfortable, she looked at her watch and exclaimed. 'Good heavens, look at the time! I must rush. Nice to see you again, enjoy the rest of your trip and have a safe flight home.' She smiled hurriedly and ducked away into the crowds, but there was a long queue at the hosiery counter, so she decided to go and have a cup of coffee before buying her tights. It would get her out of harm's way; Tony and Marianne would have left when she went back to the ground floor. She did not want to see Tony; he might ask some awkward question or talk about Nicholas.

She found a free table and sat down to drink her coffee. It was scalding hot. She stirred it absently, her eyes on the swirling black liquid. Marianne had looked fantastic, she would make Nicholas a very presentable wife. He wasn't in love with her, but their mutual fondness would make up for that. He might have second thoughts, but Stacie was sure he would eventually marry her. It would please his mother and be suitable. That was what Tony had said, and Tony was probably right; he might not have a dazzling intellect, but he was one of that family, he knew the way their world worked. It was a dynastic marriage; Marianne's family had the right sort of money and background and she had been bred and educated to marry someone like Nicholas.

Stacie stirred her coffee and thought sensibly and practically about it all; her teeth ached with the tension of not letting it hurt to imagine Nicholas marrying another girl, but she concentrated on her sane contemplation of how right Marianne was for him. She had been to the right schools, she knew the right people, she had the right attitudes and interests. She was trained to make easy, polite small talk with boring people, act as hostess at dinner parties and keep on smiling even when her head ached. Nicholas would be able to take her anywhere and be sure she would be accepted and make a good impression on his friends and business acquaintances. It was all so beautifully arranged; however hard Nicholas wriggled he was not going to get out of marrying her because everyone else wanted it, except Tony, and he didn't count, he had his own reasons for being keen to stop the marriage. Tony was jealous of his brother, he would have made a dead set at any girl who Nicholas seemed to like, maybe he had honestly convinced himself that he loved Marianne or that she wouldn't be happy with his brother. It was so easy to convince yourself of something you wanted urgently to believe to be true.

Stacie sighed, lifting the coffee cup to her lips. She had to stop thinking about it, about Nicholas. Deliberately she looked around her at the other people drinking coffee and eating Danish pastries; carrier bags and parcels piled beside them on seats or on the floor. The placed was crowded now, there wasn't a free table. Her

gaze roamed—then stopped in shock as she saw
Nicholas standing on the far side of the room. He
hadn't seen her, she thought; he was looking around
impatiently as if hunting for someone. Was he looking
for Marianne and Tony?

Her eyes absorbed every detail of his appearance
hungrily. He was wearing a dark grey overcoat today, it
made him look taller and more powerful than ever: his
black hair was windblown and his lean face carried the
flush of the cold weather, outside in the streets. Some
girls sitting near him stared, giggling admiringly.

His eyes moved along the tables on her side of the
room and Stacie's heart beat fiercely as she waited for
him to see her. She was almost frightened by the
strength of her need to meet his eyes again; she told
herself that it was a crazy physical infatuation she
would soon get over, but the craving to touch him was
so intense she was trembling. His glance passed over
her. He hadn't recognised her. Or was refusing to admit
he had? She felt sick—and then Nicholas did a double-
take, his tall body stiffening, his eyes flashed back and
she looked into them and felt her blood beating in her
ears. There was nothing around them for that instant,
they stood alone, as if on the shore of some vast sea;
she heard it surging and whispering, and a wild wind
filled her lungs with a sense of breathless freedom and
exhilaration, then Nicholas's eyes turned cold, frozen as
Arctic wastes, and the crowded room came back, the
people talking, laughing, the clatter of cutlery and clink
of cups.

She had wounded his ego; Nicholas was bitterly
angry with her. He had been telling her, that day at
Helen's, that he was attracted to her, she had got under
his skin, he had said; if he had had second sight and
known he was going to meet *her*, he would never have
asked Marianne to marry him. And then William had
appeared, and Nicholas had heard her calling him

'darling' and heard William telling her he loved her; and he had realised that she had wanted the story about Nwanda so badly simply because she wanted to give it to William. She hadn't even mentioned that there was a man in her life. William's arrival coming so fast on the heels of his own admission of an emotional involvement had been like a slap in the face. Finding out that there *was* a man would have been bad enough—but finding out that Stacie had apparently used Nicholas to get a story for William, that was the unforgivable blow. Nicholas's pride couldn't take that.

Stacie's skin was icy cold, all the colour drained out of her face, her eyes ached as though she was going to cry. Nicholas ran a slow, contemptuous stare over her and turned away. She watched him walk out of the room and was torn between relief and pain.

She waited long enough to give him time to leave the store and then got up, her coffee undrunk. Her throat hurt too much to swallow. She bought her tights and went out into the grey winter daylight. Her bus was coming, she began to run to the stop, and just got there in time to board the bus. As she was going upstairs she glanced out of the back window and briefly saw Nicholas again; he was standing beside his limousine, handing Marianne into the back seat, his long body bent in a courteous attitude.

Stacie turned away and fell into a seat. It was funny, really, she thought, one of life's bitter little jokes. She was bumping and swaying in a lumbering bus whose seats had been ripped and whose walls were scratched with crude graffiti—while Nicholas and Marianne purred away in that beautiful car. It put the whole situation in a nutshell. She was where she belonged and so were they. Their worlds had touched and spun apart again, all she had to do was forget they ever collided.

When she went back to work the following Monday she was in a mood of grim resolution. She meant to drive Nicholas out of her mind by sheer hard work. She wasn't going to have one idle moment when he could sneak back into her thoughts, if she could help it. She was lucky; they were short-staffed that week because several people had gone down with 'flu. Stacie had to do twice as much as normal. At any other time she might have complained bitterly; as it was she worked cheerfully, dashing from job to job, criss-crossing the city and back to the office and out again until she was physically weary and mentally anaesthetised.

On Tuesday morning she walked into William as she came out of the lift on the editorial floor. 'I was looking for you all morning!' he said, grinning, his face flushed and excited. 'I've got news for you! Guess who I've got an interview with tomorrow?'

She frowned. 'Who?'

'Guess,' he said, looking oddly triumphant. 'Come on, Stacie, don't be slow-witted—I'll give you a clue ... this is a very special interview, the interview of a lifetime!'

An icy shiver ran down her spine. Nicholas? she thought, and her mouth went dry. It couldn't be! He wouldn't invite William to interview him, Nicholas never gave interviews to the media—look at the way he had behaved with her! She stared at William's gleeful face and was dumb, because if Nicholas had agreed to let William interview him she was disturbed at the prospect, confused and worried by Nicholas's possible motives.

'You're being pretty slow today, darling,' William said impatiently. 'I'll give you another clue! I'm going to buy a new suit for the occasion! And a new shirt and tie. Will you come with me and advise me? I think this calls for a woman's eye. I've got to make a good impression on him. God, I'm nervous, as shaky as hell! I hope I don't blow it.' He looked hard at Stacie's dazed face. 'Stacie, I'm going to see the editor tomorrow, don't you realise what that means? If he likes me, I've got the job!'

She felt weak at the knees, but she managed a bright smile. 'That's terrific, I am pleased for you. I'm sure you'll impress him.' She must be going out of her mind. Why on earth had she jumped to such a crazy conclusion? As if Nicholas would want William to interview him! What had put such a stupid idea into her head? She had to stop thinking about him; she was becoming obsessed on the subject, whatever anybody said to her, it ended up with her thinking about Nicholas Kinsella.

'Will you come along and help me pick out a new suit?' William pressed, and she felt guilty enough to nod. She owed it to him; at least he would be getting promotion out of their relationship, even if they split up now.

'I've got to check with Ted and see if I'm down for a job this afternoon,' she said. 'Then I was going to snatch a quick lunch, but I can make do with a sandwich after you've bought your suit.'

'Meet me downstairs in the lobby in ten minutes, then?' said William, and she smiled and said that would be fine. William disappeared back into the Newsroom and Stacie walked in the opposite direction to her own department. She had been put on stand-by for the day; which meant that she had to be available to do any job that came up unexpectedly. Sometimes that left you without anything to do for hours on end, sometimes you barely stopped running from first thing in the morning until you left at night. When she appeared the Picture Editor gave her a harassed look and sorted through a little pile of yellow slips on his desk, deciding which job to send her on; it was, Stacie saw, one of those hectic days, and she wasn't sorry. She needed to keep busy.

'Hey, I've got just the job for you,' he said, grinning

suddenly and picking up one of the yellow slips. 'Your buddy Kinsella is in the City today having lunch at the Mansion House. Everyone else will be there, though. We want something a bit different. Kinsella's spending the morning at his headquarters in London Wall—grab a picture as he leaves the place and scoot back here with it.' He winked at her. 'You'll get up closer than anyone else, he obviously fancies you—get a big smile, won't you?'

'Get . . .' Stacie began furiously, and he put a hand over her lips.

'Language, language! What's a nice girl like you doing saying things like that?'

She pulled away and stormed off, very flushed, clutching the yellow slip which gave her the address in London Wall. Her stomach was in turmoil. How was she going to face Nicholas? She would have to snatch the picture and run like a hare. He mustn't see her. She would have tried to talk her boss into letting her off the hook, but she knew it would be useless. He would insist on her going and all her protests would merely make him laugh, they would be ammunition to throw at her later; he would repeat the anecodote to everyone on the paper and she would be teased out of existence. It was going to be a long time before she lived down her meeting with Nicholas Kinsella. Every time there was a picture to be taken of Nicholas, she would be favourite for the job. Agitation made her edgy as she came out of the lift on the ground floor to find William waiting for her.

'Okay?' asked William, smiling, and she flapped the little yellow slip at him.

'I've got to be at London Wall at half past twelve. I don't know if there'll be time to help you pick out a suit.' She carefully didn't mention Nicholas.

William looked at his watch. 'Oh, of course there is—it's only just gone half-past eleven. We've got plenty of time. My tailor is just across the road.' He took her arm and steered her out of the building and across between the usual dense Fleet Steeet traffic, up an alley that led to another street at the end of which was the shop William was heading for, a quiet tailor's which was luckily empty when they walked into it. William had taken Stacie's bag of equipment from her; it wasn't heavy, but it was cumbersome when you were walking fast. He greeted the smiling tailor, pushed Stacie down on a chair, dropped her bag beside her and plunged into a discussion of what he was looking for while the tailor nodded in bland understanding.

Stacie looked at her watch, her nerves jumping. It was a quarter to twelve; she watched the hands slowly ticking round and could hardly sit still. What if Nicholas saw her? She couldn't bear to see those icy eyes again, they haunted her sleep.

William was smoothing the material of one of the suits the tailor was showing him. He looked round at Stacie, his face enquiring. 'What do you think of this one?' She smiled back with an effort and said she liked it. William went into the fitting room and Stacie watched the minutes ticking past while she waited for him to emerge. He came out, grimacing. The suit wasn't a perfect fit, he didn't have time to have it altered, he told the tailor. William was a standard size, so the tailor quickly produced other suits to fit him.

It was twenty minutes before he found a suit he liked which fitted perfectly; a smooth grey pinstripe with an elegant, tight-fitting waistcoat. Stacie admired it enthusiastically, refusing to look at her watch again. If she was late and missed Nicholas it would be too bad. Her boss might shriek with fury, but she had a good excuse; the traffic was appalling. William was delighted by her reaction to the suit; he was very pleased with life today. He had wanted her there to be an admiring audience, she realised. His ego needed the boost of having someone there to applaud him because in spite of his self-confident manner William was secretly nervous about this interview. So much hung on it; although he would never admit to nerves, he was showing off like a little boy whistling in the dark to keep his spirits up.

'Come out with me tomorrow night?' he asked as they stood on the pavement trying to hail a taxi for her. 'Whether I get the job or not I'll want to live it up afterwards. A celebration—or a wake, what does it matter? We'll have a special dinner and go on to Stringfellows to dance, okay?'

'I'd love to,' she said, because she couldn't refuse. William had to go into this interview feeling like a winner, Stacie couldn't let him down.

He kissed her as a taxi screeched to a halt beside them. 'You're terrific, do you know that? It makes me feel good just knowing you're cheering for me.'

She got into the taxi feeling two inches tall and sank back into the corner of the cab. It was sickening to keep pretending that nothing had changed, but what else could she do at the moment? This wasn't the time to tell William that she didn't want to see him any more, it was over, goodbye. She liked him too much to hurt him like that just when he most needed support; she did want him to get that job, she wanted William to be happy and successful, she dreaded the thought of his bewilderment when she faded out of his life for good. Stacie hated feeling like a hypocrite; her instinct was to be frank and straightforward, not to lie and pretend and hide her real feelings.

It was just as well people couldn't see inside your head, she thought, staring at the back of the taxi-driver's head. She had often wondered what it would be like if someone had the power to read your thoughts. Telepathy was a scary idea; to be able to retreat into your own private world where nobody could reach you was essential. What if other people could eavesdrop on your thoughts? It would be the end of all personal privacy. The inside of a human mind was the last sure stronghold of the individual; these days you could find your house bugged, your most private conversations recorded, your telephone tapped, but they hadn't yet invented a machine that could tap your unspoken thoughts. No doubt it was on their agenda for the future, she thought grimly. Maybe Nicholas Kinsella had good reason for surrounding himself with security men; a lot of people would love to know what *he* talked about in private.

The taxi dropped her outside the address she had been given and she stood on the pavement staring up at the building, which was a typical modern structure: glass and concrete, without charm or beauty, and with very little personality. Stacie made a face at it. You could see buildings like that anywhere in the modern world; towering above city centres, oppressing everything human with the dead hand of functionalism. They reminded her of man-made anthills, teeming with soulless activity: human beings walked past her as she waited in the street, went into one of the stony structures rising on each side of her and became living micro-chips in a vast calculating machine. The city throbbed and buzzed with power, the traffic flowed jerkily along the tarmac between the buildings; Stacie felt depressed and tense as she watched the plate glass windows and doors of Nicholas's London office. A great brass plate was screwed to the marble facing alongside the main door. Kinsella-Moell International, she read, keeping her distance. Nicholas was inside there, he belonged in that glittering, inhuman world, he was the master of it.

A quick glance at her watch told her it was now past the time at which he was supposed to leave for the Mansion House. Perhaps she had missed him, he had gone out through another door or left early? Painful relief spread through her, she crossed over the street and was about to walk back towards the nearest tube station, which was a few minutes away, when a group of men came through the main door of Nicholas's office block. Something in the way they moved caught her attention. Her eyes hastily skimmed their faces, but Nicholas wasn't among them and Stacie would have walked on if she hadn't suddenly recognised Roughton.

He was in the centre of the group; stolid in a belted black leather coat, his pugnacious face lifted as his eyes watched the upper floors of the buildings opposite. Puzzled, Stacie watched him. A long black limousine drove up and edged into a parking space exactly outside the Kinsella-Moell building. Roughton glanced at it, nodding to the driver—and then he suddenly saw Stacie.

He did a double-take, his eyes narrowing and his heavy body stiffening. He took a step towards her and the men with him immediately looked round and then stared across the road at her, too. They were all wearing the same tense, alert, watchful expression.

What on earth were they doing? Stacie wondered. It was too late for her to duck out of sight or pretend that she just happened to be strolling casually along this street, so she unzipped her bag and got out her camera, trying to look calm and sure of herself. This wasn't an isolated country road; Roughton and his buddies wouldn't dare to act tough with her in a busy London street.

One of the men with Roughton spoke to him in a low voice. She couldn't catch what he said, but she saw Roughton answering, his expression uncertain. They both looked at her a second later and she guessed that they had been debating what to do about her. As they didn't move in her direction she stayed where she was, her camera strap around her neck, ready to take a rapid picture of Nicholas when he finally appeared. Catching

Roughton's eye a moment later, she gave him a
mocking little smile. She was right—he didn't dare to
hustle her out here with so many eye-witnesses.
Roughton didn't like that taunting provocation; he
scowled the way he had when she called him a gorilla.

The plate-glass doors swung open again and her
pulses went crazy as she saw Nicholas coming out. He
strode across the pavement, his black head gleaming as
a shaft of wintry sunshine hit it. Stacie's hands were
trembling as she focused on his face. The picture might
be blurred, but she could blame that on the fact that he
had been moving. When she had taken a couple of
pictures she turned to run before Roughton or one of
the others could catch her and grab her camera away;
and as she did so she saw something glint in a car down
the street.

At any other time she might not have realised what
she had seen, but with Roughton on the other side of
the road some subliminal association of ideas made her
mind work with the speed of light. It only took a split
second for her to identify it; that glint had been cold
sunlight flashing over the barrel of a gun.

Someone in a parked car further down the street had
a gun trained on Nicholas, and she remembered the
threats made by Nwanda's rebels, she knew why
Roughton and his friends had been fanning out across
the pavement walking with crab-like wariness, staring
all around them, why Nicholas was moving so fast as he
headed for his car. Terror made her heart stop and then
begin thudding violently.

It could only have taken her a few seconds to work it
all out, and she acted instinctively almost at once;
running across the road towards Nicholas, hardly
conscious of screaming his name.

He paused, about to get into his car, staring over the
top of it at her, a hand flat on the black metal. Stacie
screamed: 'No, no, get down! There's a man with a gun . . .'

The next instant everything was in a state of panic and confusion; she heard the whine of a bullet and saw Nicholas's security men moving. Nicholas vanished as some of his men threw themselves on him, covering him as he fell with their own bodies. Stacie had almost reached the limousine when something struck her in the back with the violence of a kick from a horse, hurling her sideways. She fell between two parked cars. Her head hit the kerb and she lay, dazed with shock, too numb to feel pain. Bullets hit the cars beside her; whining metallically as they scarred paintwork and smashed windows. Glass sprayed everywhere. People ran, screaming, along the pavement in front of her, but she couldn't move, she lay in the gutter, her mind quite blank, and couldn't remember what had happened, she didn't know where she was or what all the noise meant.

She had a feeling she should force herself up; there was something she had to do, something she needed urgently to know, but she couldn't remember what it was or why it mattered so much. It hurt to move, but Stacie had an obstinate, tenacious willpower, she forced her head up and tried to crawl. Something was running warmly down her face—it felt like tears, and she thought irritably: 'Why am I crying?' The wetness splashed on to her hand and she focused on it just before she lost consciousness. It was bright red. Blood! she thought, and was stupidly surprised.

CHAPTER NINE

STACIE could hear bells; they clanged and reverberated all around her. It must be Sunday, she thought, frowning, but it hurt when her forehead wrinkled, so she let her face become blank again while she tried to gather the energy to open her eyes. That didn't seem a good idea, though: if it was Sunday, why not stay in bed and catch up on some sleep? she told herself. She felt so tired, as if she hadn't slept at all. She couldn't remember ever feeling this tired before, it would be wonderful to go back to sleep. But she knew there was some very urgent reason why she had to wake up. There was something she had to do, but she couldn't think: those bells kept ringing, why didn't they stop? She moved agitatedly, and a hand caught hold of her fingers as they twisted about restlessly.

'Stacie . . .' A voice was saying something in an inaudible husky mutter; the words floated away before she could catch them, but she felt the firm grip of the hand on her own and with a tremendous effort she forced her lids up.

There was a blurred unreality about what she saw; it reminded her of being at the dentist after she had had a tooth out. She saw white metallic walls, a white ceiling, very low, someone in white sitting beside her, but all very dimly—it was so strange that she couldn't speak, she just stared around, and then there was a face she did recognise, but what was it doing here? Obviously she was still asleep and dreaming; what else explained the ringing and the strange little white room which seemed to be moving along at great speed?

'How do you feel, Stacie?' Nicholas Kinsella asked, his thumb smoothing the back of her hand.

'Stay out of my dreams, damn you—can't I get away from you?' she said clearly, and shut her eyes. This time it was easy to go back to sleep; she just floated away feeling at peace. The urgency had gone.

The next time she woke up she was lying flat on her stomach. It was very quiet around her, she listened to the silence and in it heard someone else breathing. Stacie shifted her head, wincing slightly, and at once the person in the room moved.

'Hallo, keep still. You've had an accident and you're in hospital.' There was a girl's face bending over her. Stacie stared, listening, and the white-capped nurse smiled at her. 'Don't worry, you're going to be fine. You had surgery, that's all, but you mustn't move yet, and I'm afraid you must stay on your front for a day or two.'

Stacie moistened her lips with the tip of her tongue. Her mouth was dry. 'Could I have a drink?' she whispered, and the nurse filled a glass with water and held the glass to her lips. Stacie drank thirstily, still half stupid with sleep; or was it drugs? she wondered. She seemed to be having difficulty concentrating, her mind was slow-moving and she couldn't remember much. The nurse took the glass away and Stacie saw a hypodermic in her hand a moment later. As the girl pulled back the bedclothes Stacie protested weakly. She didn't want whatever was in that thing.

'It won't hurt,' the girl said patronisingly, as though she was three years old. She rubbed at Stacie's skin with a piece of cottonwool and almost at once Stacie was resentfully closing her eyes again, the frown on her face smoothing out.

Her parents visited her next day; Stacie was more or less normal, although she was still being given regular drugs to control the pain of her wounded shoulder. She had been allowed to sit up against a bank of pillows which cushioned her in the small of the back and made sure her shoulder wasn't put under any pressure. That side of her body was thickly bandaged and she had another bandage around her head. When she first noticed that she thought she must have been shot there, too, but apparently she had hit her head on the edge of the kerb when she fell. She remembered her surprise when she saw the blood splash on to her hand. She remembered everything now, including that dreamlike trip in the ambulance with the bell ringing and Nicholas beside her. She didn't remember her operation.

She hadn't asked the nurse many questions, but: 'Was Mr Kinsella hurt in the shooting?' had been almost the first, and she had been silent with relief when the girl assured her that he hadn't been hit by any of the bullets.

'You were lucky,' the nurse had told her, smiling. 'The bullet lodged in your shoulder, it had to be removed during the operation—but it missed any vital organs, it's only a flesh wound.'

'What do you mean—only? It hurts like hell,' Stacie said.

'We must tell Doctor, then, mustn't we?' said the nurse in that kindergarten voice into which she slipped all too readily.

'Is that the royal plural or am I included?' Stacie enquired, and the girl looked blank.

'Sorry?' she asked questioningly.

'So I should think,' Stacie said. 'What happened to the other guys? The ones with the guns?'

'You can read all about it later,' the nurse said, rustling the newspaper she had been reading and grinning. 'You're quite a heroine!'

'Oh, no! Not again!' When she got back to work, Stacie realised, she was going to come in for some pretty heavy teasing about this further escapade. It wouldn't have mattered if Nicholas Kinsella hadn't been involved—but as he was, people were going to talk, and she shuddered at the idea of what they would say.

'We'll have to ask Doctor before you can read it,' the
nurse said, and looked disbelieving when Stacie grimly
declined the offer. She did not want to read about
herself in the newspapers; she felt like someone trapped
in a spotlight and unable to run from the thousands of
unknown staring eyes. Everyone would be speculating
about her and Nicholas now; the first incident had been
entirely professional, but this time was different. It
would look as if she saw more of him than she would in
any professional capacity; it was bound to cause gossip.
It was too big a coincidence.

When her parents arrived they carried a basket of
fruit, flowers and a pile of newspapers which they
dropped on to her bedside cabinet with meaningful
smiles.

'Helen will be up to see you tomorrow,' said Mrs
Murray, kissing her. 'She wanted to come yesterday,
but the hospital said you couldn't have visitors, you
were still groggy after your operation and wouldn't
know any of us anyway. Roland told Helen they were
right—well, he should know. He said we should wait
until you could talk.' While she was chattering away
Mrs Murray was looking at Stacie closely. She sighed,
smiling. 'You're a bit pale, but you look much better
than I thought you would. Is it very painful, dear?'

Whenever Stacie saw her mother she could imagine
Helen in twenty years' time; the resemblance, both
mental and physical, was extraordinary, and you could
see the same process happening with Helen's twins,
especially Ann. Mrs Murray was energetic, managing,
warm-hearted and inclined to know best for everyone
around her.

'Oh, I'll live,' Stacie said lightly, and her father smiled
at her. George Murray was a quiet man, he hadn't said
much since he walked into the small hospital room, he
never did have much to say, but when he spoke people
usually listened. Spare and grey-haired, he had calm

eyes which noticed everything. He had a passion for lonely pursuits; fished on his local river and spent hours in the hills near his home, bird-watching, an interest he had passed on to Roland. They got on well together; in many ways they were rather similar, even to having the same dry, understated sense of humour. Stacie had sometimes wondered if Helen hadn't picked out Roland from her other boy-friends simply because he had some of her father's calm authority, his gentle firmness.

'You're in all the newspapers,' her mother said excitedly. 'I'm making a scrapbook of the cuttings.' She picked one of the pile of papers up and offered it to Stacie. 'They all have a picture of you being carried into the ambulance.'

'Your mother cried when she saw it,' Mr Murray told her, and his wife bridled.

'I did not! Anyone would be horrified. All that blood . . .' She stopped, looking quickly at Stacie. 'Of course, it was only a flesh wound, it bled more than . . .'

'Must we talk about it?' Stacie interrupted, frowning. She knew she had lost a lot of blood; she had noticed the transfusion stand beside her bed on the first night. It had made her shudder, she hated the sight of the red blood dripping slowly through the plastic, it was too gruesome, something out of science fiction. The idea of losing blood made her feel weak and helpless, and she couldn't bear to be either.

'It was such a terrible shock,' Mrs Murray said. 'When Mr Kinsella rang I wanted to get the first train to London. I was in such a state . . .'

'Nicholas rang you?' Stacie was startled into using his first name, and only realised what she had done when she saw her parents staring and then saw them exchange a look which made her go a scalded pink.

'He's been so kind,' Mrs Murray told her. 'He insisted on booking us into a hotel and we've got the most lovely suite, I've never stayed anywhere like it in

my life and they can't do enough for us, it's obvious
that Mr Kinsella told them to take special care of us,
and when we arrived he'd sent me the most beautiful
flowers, a huge display of roses and carnations and such
a kind card, and he's asked us to have dinner, and
Helen's invited too. She's arriving later this afternoon.
Roland couldn't get the time off and they had to
arrange for someone to look after the children so Helen
couldn't get away until today, but the hospital said you
shouldn't have too many visitors at first, just us to
begin with, and she can see you tomorrow, but we're
having dinner with Mr Kinsella tonight, he said to call
him Nicholas, but I can't get used to that, I said to
Helen: are you sure you aren't dreaming it up, you
know what an imagination she's got, I don't know
where she gets it from, but for once she isn't, obviously.
I must say, you're very secretive, Stacie, but then you
always were, you get it from your father.'

George Murray waited until his wife paused for
breath, and then said gently: 'We mustn't tire Stacie,
must we, dear? You know what the Sister said.'

They both stared at Stacie, who was as pale as the
pillows against which she was propped. She had
absorbed the high, excited tone of her mother's voice,
the flush in her face, the brightness of her eyes, and
adding that to everything Mrs Murray had said about
Nicholas she was disturbed.

'I don't know what you think I'm being secretive
about,' she said slowly. 'But if it is Mr Kinsella, don't
jump to any conclusions, because . . .' She broke off,
frowning. How could she phrase it? They hadn't asked
any direct questions she could answer. 'There are . . . no
conclusions to jump to,' she ended with embarrassment.

Mrs Murray beamed complacently. 'We're not going
to pry, Stacie. You'll tell us in your own good time.'

'There's nothing to tell!' Stacie insisted, and her
father stared hard at her. She looked at him pleadingly.

'Dad, don't let her get the wrong idea!' It was horrifying to imagine her mother burbling on at Nicholas the way she had just talked about him. No doubt Nicholas was grateful to Stacie for warning him, she might possibly have saved his life, and she had been shot herself in the process, which more than explained why he was going to so much trouble to be pleasant to her parents. He was a very rich man; it wouldn't mean much to him to install her family in an expensive hotel suite and send them flowers and take them to dinner, but to her mother it all had a very different motive. Helen must have put the idea into her head, of course; incurably romantic, Helen preferred the brightly coloured world of her fantasy to the real life motives which had prompted Nicholas to do so much for Stacie's family. But it would be embarrassing for Nicholas when he realised what construction the Murrays were putting on his actions. Stacie was glad she wouldn't be there. She loved her mother and she loved her sister, but sometimes she could strangle both of them.

'Don't upset yourself,' said George Murray, patting her hand comfortingly. 'I'll make sure we're all discreet at dinner.'

'I'm always discreet,' Mrs Murray protested, looking offended. 'What on earth do you mean, George? As if I'd say anything out of place! Good heavens . . .'

Stacie closed her eyes, she felt very tired again. It was a strain talking to people, her shoulder was throbbing.

Her father kissed her cheek. 'We're going now, we'll come again tomorrow afternoon. Helen will be here in the morning. They have said we must take it in turns, only two visitors at a time or it will tire you.'

She opened her eyes again and managed a smile for him. Her mother kissed her, too, and asked if there was anything she needed. 'One of your own nighties? That hospital thing is so starchy, it can't be comfortable.'

When they had gone the nurse came back with the

doctor and Stacie suffered another examination. 'You're doing splendidly,' the middle-aged doctor told her cheerfully. 'Healthy girl, good recovery, out of here in no time. Meal tonight if you're good.' He bounced out of the room and the nurse gave Stacie an approving smile.

'We'll have a sleep now, shall we?'

'Is there room for both of us on this bed?' Stacie asked, and closed her eyes. She slept lightly and kept starting awake from a nightmare about bullets whining over her head and glass crashing all around her while she crawled blindly towards a safety she knew was just ahead although she couldn't reach it. Once when she woke up she was sure she heard breathing in the room and thought the nurse was sitting there again, but as she opened her eyes to look she heard the door close. She was aware of a raging thirst. She groped for the cord which held a bell close to her hand and rang firmly. After a moment the door opened and the nurse came to the bed, looking anxious.

'Did he disturb you?'

'What?' Stacie stared at her. 'Who?'

The nurse looked self-conscious, flushing. 'Oh, nothing—why did you ring?'

'I wanted a drink,' Stacie explained. 'Was it the doctor?'

The nurse poured some water and held it to her mouth without answering. 'Go back to sleep,' she said, and tucked the bedclothes around Stacie in a firm manner which meant she wouldn't answer any more questions.

Stacie slept for several hours and when she woke up she was very hungry. It was a slightly deceptive hunger, though, because when they brought her a supper tray she could only manage some of the delicious beef consommé and a few forkfuls of the omelette which followed it, and she felt lightheaded as she settled back against her pillows. The nurse removed her tray, brushed her hair and washed her hands and face, as if she was a two-year-old; Stacie couldn't have done it for herself, she was still too weak, but she resented it, childishly.

'Up to another visitor?' the nurse asked. 'I don't think so, do you? We're rather tired again, aren't we?' It was true, but Stacie did not like having all her decisions made for her, and she bristled from head to foot, scowling, her eyes truculent.

'I'm fine, I'd like to have visitors.' And put that into the royal plural, if you like! she thought, eyeing the nurse disagreeably. She wasn't much more than twenty-two, in spite of her nanny-like manner, and Stacie had had enough of being heaved about and babied by someone so much younger than herself. Her mind might reasonably point out that the girl put on her air of sure authority with her uniform to make sure of being taken seriously, but Stacie was in the irritable mood of someone who dislikes being ill and resents being unable to help themselves.

She could hear the visitors walking past along the corridor. This was a private wing of the hospital and very quiet normally. Stacie had already begun to know the daily routine which began with first light when the night nurses came along with their trolleys to take temperatures and hand out teas. She watched the nurse walk to the door and open it.

'You can come in now,' the girl said to someone, and Mrs Kinsella walked through the door carrying an enormous spray of flowers sheathed in a transparent envelope.

'Oh, aren't they lovely?' the nurse enthused eagerly. 'We're being spoilt—this room is like a flower shop!' Her round eyes were not on the flowers, however, they were riveted on Mrs Kinsella's long sable coat which rippled silkily as she walked towards Stacie, on a wave of expensive French perfume and with a guilty, uneasy

smile that kept vanishing. Mrs Kinsella awkwardly
handed Stacie the bouquet, as her hand brushed Stacie's
fingers, they both smiled in the same self-conscious,
nervous way.

'My hands are cold, I'm afraid,' Mrs Kinsella said at
exactly the same time as Stacie muttered: 'Thank you,
what beautiful flowers, it's very kind of you.'

The nurse came and took them before Stacie had had
time to do more than glance at them through their
polythene covering; they were hothouse blooms, white
chrysanthemeums as big as plates, with curled petals in
deep layers, pink carnations and yellow rosebuds with
long, long stems.

'I'll put them in water, shall I?' said the nurse, backing
with her gaze still on Mrs Kinsella's ravishing coat.

The door shut and Mrs Kinsella perched on the edge
of a chair. 'How do you feel?' she asked Stacie brightly.

'Very well, thank you.' Stacie felt like a polite
schoolgirl up before the headmistress for some nameless
deed; she couldn't quite meet Mrs Kinsella's eyes. What
was she doing here?

'I had to come,' Mrs Kinsella burst out, her fingers
twisting together among the dark brown fur of her coat.
'I had to thank you, myself. So brave! If you hadn't . . .
I . . . it doesn't bear thinking about . . . and you might
have been . . . thank God it was only . . . and after all I
said to you . . . I don't know what to say, I'm ashamed
of myself.'

'Please!' Stacie muttered, very red. 'Anyone would
have . . .'

'No, no, don't make light of it,' Mrs Kinsella insisted
huskily. 'You saved his life, if you hadn't shouted to
him he would have been hit by that first bullet it
missed him by a whisker, he said. If he hadn't turned to
look at you it would have gone straight through his
forehead.' She broke off, swallowing, and Stacie took a
painful breath, going white.

She felt a blinding stab of terror at the realisation of how close to death Nicholas had been, how close to it he must always be, walking in the lethal glitter of his power. How could he bear it? How could his mother bear it? Stacie knew she would never sleep at night if someone she loved was in such constant danger.

I can't love him, she thought in anguish. It would mean too much pain, I would never have a quiet hour; too much would always threaten our love—their personal world would be ringed with enemies intent on destroying whatever happiness they did achieve, and Stacie refused to risk that ever-present threat.

'Why isn't he more careful?' she said angrily, and Mrs Kinsella leaned closer, sighing.

'Do you think I haven't said that to him? Nicholas can be so pigheaded and he never tells me anything— just like his father, that's where he learnt it. He keeps his problems to himself and thinks he's doing me a favour, he thinks he's protecting me.' She looked at the bulky outline under Stacie's hospital nightdress and frowned. 'Is your shoulder very painful? Nicholas has been very worried, I've hardly set eyes on him since it happened. But don't worry, my dear—you can have plastic surgery to remove any scars. In a few months there'll be no sign of what happened. You'll be able to wear a bikini without a qualm.'

Stacie forced a polite smile—it hadn't even occurred to her that she might have any lasting disfigurement from the wound and she didn't find the idea of going through plastic surgery very appealing, either, but she hid her reaction, and changed the subject.

'Is it cold tonight?'

'Freezing,' said Mrs Kinsella, smoothing her sable coat with a fond hand. 'They say we shall have snow tomorrow, and I believe them. The temperature has dropped like a stone. They're getting bad weather in the

States, I hear—friends tell me it's been snowing a blizzard in New York. I don't think I'll hurry home.'

Stacie nodded, pleating the white honeycomb coverlet on her bed and watching her fingers as though fascinated by them. 'Is Marianne still with you?'

'Of course,' Mrs Kinsella said stiffly.

Of course, thought Stacie, suppressing a wry smile. Why had she bothered to ask? It might be cold outside, but in here the temperature had dropped very suddenly in spite of the hospital's heavy central heating. Mentioning Marianne had reminded Mrs Kinsella of things she had forgotten in her gratitude to Stacie.

'You look tired, my dear, I'd better leave you to rest.' Mrs Kinsella stood up, hovering as though not quite sure how to get out of the room. Stacie looked up with a rueful smile.

'It was good of you to visit me, thank you for the flowers.' Mrs Kinsella's hair shone in the strip lighting like spun silver; she seemed more grey than she had been before. The shock of the attempt on Nicholas had aged her visibly; her face was drawn and lined. It must be a constant burden to worry about her son's safety, Stacie could sympathise with her about that.

'Nonsense, it was nothing ... I'm so grateful ... thank you for ...' Mrs Kinsella was incoherent again; she made a little dart at Stacie and kissed her cheek. 'Thank you.'

When she had gone the small room still held the ghost of her perfume: delicately clinging to Stacie's hair and skin. Stacie sighed, feeling weary and depressed. She liked Nicholas's mother more now than she had done; they had come close to understanding each other when they talked about him, but Stacie knew that the wall had come up between them the instant she mentioned Marianne. Mrs Kinsella might be grateful to her for helping to save Nicholas's life, but in other ways she had not changed.

There was no point in thinking about it. It made no
real difference what Mrs Kinsella thought or wanted—
Stacie knew there was no future for her with someone
like Nicholas, she wouldn't think about him.

She stretched out a hand and carefully picked up one
of the newspapers her parents had brought her. It was
difficult to move her arms; it made her shoulder throb
fiercely. She skimmed over the front page story about
the assassination attempt, wincing at some of the purple
prose devoted to herself. They had got her age wrong
and spelt her name with a y. It was silly to be so
irritated, but she liked Stacie the way she spelt it. She
wasn't surprised by the stupid little mistakes; they were
the norm in popular journalism.

For the first time she discovered that the two
assassins had been killed. She frowned in shock as she
read the description of how their car had ploughed into
the window of a supermarket and burst into flames.
Luckily no shopper had been injured; apart from the
two men in the car the only injury suffered had been by
a young passer-by who had been cut by flying glass.
During the original shooting incident, though, one of
Nicholas's security men had been slightly wounded in
the hand and a car driving past had crashed, injuring
the driver, who was said to be comfortable, in hospital,
although a number of other people had been taken to
hospital suffering from shock.

Stacie found the pictures which accompanied the
story even more distressing; the narrow street looked
like a disaster area, cars slewed across the road, broken
glass littering the pavement, ambulances lined up and
policemen everywhere. In one of the pictures she saw
herself on a stretcher, her face totally unfamiliar with
the bloodstains smeared across it, being lifted into the
back of an ambulance. Nicholas was there, caught in
profile; he looked different, grey, older, shocked. She
stared at his face and trembled convulsively. He had so

nearly died; she couldn't bear to think of it. She let the paper drop and lay back, eyes closed. Inside her head she was seeing him as she had seen him when she screamed his name in terror. 'Nicholas!' It all came back, drowning her, she was shaking from head to foot and icy cold, her teeth were chattering.

The night nurse walked in a moment later, took one look at her and ran for the doctor. Stacie looked at him blankly as he rolled up her nightdress sleeve. She felt as if she was floating above the bed, every separate nerve in her body was jangling violently. The needle went in and the doctor gave her a professional look. 'Don't worry, it's only delayed shock,' he said casually, and she felt angry because she had never felt so ill in her life, how dared he talk as if it was a mere nothing? Couldn't he see how ill she was?

He picked up the newspaper, looked at it with one brow lifted. 'Now what idiot let you see that?' he asked, but he was looking at the nurse, who bridled.

'I didn't give it to her, doctor. Someone must have brought it in—I can't search them, can I? People will do these things.'

He tut-tutted. 'Very silly!'

Stacie had drifted away, she heard their voices and didn't care what they were saying; her pulses were calming and her body was picking up a little warmth again as she relaxed and stopped that terrible shaking. She had never been so glad to slip into sleep; she dived into it like someone diving into a warm, warm sea.

She woke up in darkness and at once knew there was someone in the room with her, as she had known last time, from the careful sound of breathing. She lay still, listening; unalarmed because she believed it was a nurse, she had become used to finding a nurse at her bedside when she woke. After a moment she closed her eyes again, too tired to talk, and fell back into sleep, but this time her sleep was troubled by dreams. She was

standing in the street watching Nicholas; bullets whined
around her and she tried to warn him, to get to him,
but she couldn't move, her feet were rooted to the
ground, she couldn't even scream. Her mouth opened
soundlessly, she struggled in panic and terror, her
heart pounding so hard it felt as if it would come
bursting through her heaving ribs. At last the spell
broke and she could move, could scream. 'Nicholas, no,
no . . .'

She was sitting up in the darkness, sweating,
trembling, for a moment unable to remember where she
was, and then she felt someone's arms holding her and
a hand stroked her hair, a voice whispered: 'Ssh . . .
you're safe, Stacie, you're safe, I've got you.'

She couldn't see his face, it was too shadowy in the
little room. She looked disbelievingly at him, but she
leaned on his strength, still shuddering, filled with a
blinding sense of joy because he was alive, they hadn't
killed him.

'I dreamt you were being killed and I couldn't stop it,
I couldn't move—it was like being paralysed, it was
going to happen and I couldn't do anything,' she
whispered in a rapid, breathless voice. 'I was going
mad; it was terrible!'

'Ssh,' he said, kissing her hair. 'It's over, it didn't
happen. You're quite safe now.' He brushed his lips
over her eyes. 'Go back to sleep, darling.'

She shivered. 'I couldn't. I can't bear that dream
again. I keep dreaming it. It's so terrifying, not being
able to do anything.'

'I'll put the light on and get the nurse to give you
something,' Nicholas said, moving as if to release her,
and she put her arm around his neck to hold him.

'Not yet. I don't want the light on yet.' Once she
could see him, once the light had broken into the
intimate darkness holding them, it would be over and
she would have to be sane and rational and tell him not

to come here again. She couldn't see him, mustn't see him, it would only make it harder.

Nicholas gently laid her back on the pillows. 'Does your shoulder hurt?' he asked, stroking her hair very softly, and she wanted to tell him the truth—that it didn't hurt as much as the touch of his hand, that was quite unbearable; she wanted him to go on stroking her hair and kissing her, but it was only the stupidity of being half-drugged and unable to control her own folly.

'What are you *doing* here?' she whispered.

'Visiting you,' he said drily.

'Why?' she asked, meaning: why when I am asleep? Why not, when I'm awake?

'You told me in no uncertain terms that you didn't want to see me,' he said in a flat voice. 'So I've been coming in for a few minutes when I knew you weren't conscious.'

Stacie was silent, remembering several times when she had woken up with the distinct impression that someone had just left the room.

'Shall I call the nurse now?' he asked, and switched on the light. Stacie blinked like an owl, knowing she looked terrible, her hair must be tousled and her face hadn't a trace of make-up. The hospital nightgown wasn't the most seductive garment in the world, either. Looking at her like this wouldn't make any man's heart miss a beat.

'I don't want any more sleeping pills,' she said. 'I feel as though my head was stuffed with cottonwool as it is . . .'

'You need to sleep,' Nicholas said gently, frowning.

'I know I look terrible,' she said with despair because she wanted so much to look gorgeous when he saw her, and she hated to have him look at her when she was in such a mess.

Nicholas looked at her, stared: his grey eyes brilliant and the pupils obsidian, glittering, black, enlarged with feeling. Then he smiled.

'You look beautiful,' he said in a voice so deep it made her throat close in shock. He picked up one of her hands and his black head bent over it while she watched in stricken silence. She felt his mouth press into her palm and her heart hurt inside her.

'Don't!' she said harshly, pulling her hand away. 'You mustn't! Oh, can't you see how impossible it is? It's out of the question. I can't—you can't!' Her stammered words broke off with a smothered sob, she turned her head away, rubbing a hand over her wet eyes. 'Please go away,' she whispered shakily.

Nicholas stood up, slowly. 'I'm not going to apologise for loving you,' he said in a quiet voice. 'I owe you my life—that gives me the right to love you now. I think you're wrong about this, but maybe I'm prejudiced, I'm kidding myself that you'd be happier with me. I don't think I am, but then I wouldn't, I suppose. If you love him . . . think you do . . . you must marry him, there's nothing I can do to stop you, obviously, but for your own sake, Stacie, wait, don't rush into anything. I don't know you very well yet, but I think I know you better than you may think. You knew him first, that's all.' He sighed, shifting his feet. 'This isn't the time to talk about it, you're so weak still. But I can't let you rush into a marriage which I'm certain isn't right for you. All I want you to do is promise to wait and give it time.'

Stacie had listened to him in confused bewilderment at first, until it dawned on her that he thought she was going to marry William and that her rejection of him was entirely due to that. As she listened she realised she couldn't disillusion him; he must never know why she was unwilling to get seriously involved or he would pressure her to change her mind. He was being gentle with her now because she was ill, but Nicholas was not the man to accept a rejection easily. Once she was on her feet and completely recovered, he would be back and next time the pressure would be intolerable.

Huskily she said: 'I won't change my mind, Nicholas. Please, just leave me alone.' She closed her eyes and tears crawled out from under her lids; she could have held them back, but she chose to let them escape. She wanted Nicholas to go quickly; she couldn't bear any more.

There was a silence, then he bent and kissed her hair. The next minute he had gone, and then the tears quickened and Stacie couldn't stop them, they ran down her face like a river.

CHAPTER TEN

WILLIAM visited her several days later. Stacie was sitting up in bed reading a magazine; she wasn't expecting visitors because both Helen and her parents had left London, at her insistence; although they hadn't even hinted at it, she had guessed that they wanted to get home. Helen hated being away from her children and their parents found London exhausting after the tranquillity of their Northumberland hills. When the usual tramp of visiting feet went past her door Stacie heard them without expectation, so when someone paused outside and she heard the door handle turning her heart skipped a beat and she looked up tensely, her fingers gripping the magazine.

'Oh, hallo, William!' she said, recognising him and conscious of both relief and disappointment. 'Come in!'

He came over and handed her a large box of black grapes, smiling rather stiffly. She thanked him and took a grape while he asked how she was and she told him she was fine, now, thanks. William sat down on the edge of the chair by her bed and unzipped the leather jacket he wore; he looked uneasy, but then people always feel uneasy in hospital.

'I tried to see you days ago,' he suddenly burst out. 'They wouldn't let me in—said I wasn't on their list of permitted visitors. I suppose I can guess who drew that list up?'

Stacie felt herself colour and was shaken by the terse tone. 'I think I was only allowed to see my family,' she protested unsteadily.

'And Nicholas Kinsella!' accused William, and Stacie hurriedly offered him the grapes, saying they were

174

delicious, try one, they were the best grapes she had ever eaten.

'Don't keep me in suspense,' she said as he took a grape, frowning at her. 'Did you get the job? Or don't you know yet?'

He was distracted at once, as everyone is by talk of themselves, he stopped scowling and began smiling, brightening. 'I got it!'

'Oh, that's terrific!' Stacie was delighted for him, she smiled back warmly.

'I only heard yesterday—the letter took four days to reach me, isn't that crazy? Four days! I'd decided I hadn't got it and I'd started wondering if I ought to find another job, I couldn't work under Gerry after this—and then the letter came.' He ate grapes as he talked, his face alight with excitement, and Stacie told him how glad she was, he had been the only one for the job and the editor had had the sense to see that. William beamed and decided she deserved to hear a blow-by-blow account of his interview with the editor. It took him a good ten minutes, and he didn't leave out a syllable of his own brilliant remarks or the editor's impressed responses.

'I had a long chat with Atkins, too,' he said. 'He's happy with the idea of me in the job now.' William had obviously pledged his loyalty to the empire-building Atkins, Stacie concluded, listening wryly. Well, it was the only wise thing to do.

'Atkins wanted me to write a piece on you for the paper,' William said suddenly, and she looked at him in shock. He grinned at her. 'I told him politely to shove off. Atkins tried to visit you, too—did you know?'

She hadn't and stared, shaking her head.

'He couldn't get past the dragon, either. For a while this place was knee-deep in pressmen trying to see you. The porter had to drag two photographers off the wall. They were trying to get pictures of you through the window.'

'My God,' Stacie said helplessly. 'The paparazzi—
how ironic!'

William laughed. 'Well, that's show business. Atkins
used an old picture of you that I managed to dig up.'
He grimaced. 'They cut me off, though—symbolic, isn't
it?'

Stacie tensed, looking away, and William asked in a
flat voice: 'It is true that Kinsella's paying all your bills
and spends a lot of time here, isn't it?'

'Where did you hear that?' Stacie was startled into
looking up. Helen had let it out that Nicholas was
paying for this private room and all her treatment, but
she didn't know how the papers had got hold of that.

'The whole of Fleet Street knows. You know the way
they work. Heaven knows who told them, they paid
someone who works here, I suppose.' William moodily
ate another grape in tiny nibbles. 'How much fire is
there behind all the smoke?'

'I don't know what you're talking about,' she fenced.

'Don't worry, I won't repeat a word of what you
say—but if it is true, if Kinsella's interest is personal,
don't you think I ought to be told?'

Stacie didn't know what to say to him, she stared at
the wall, biting her lip. William waited for a minute,
then said: 'Okay, let's do it another way. You tell me
that there isn't a word of truth in all the stories the
gossip columns are printing, and I'll believe you.'

Stacie couldn't lie to him, she sat in silence, and as
that silence dragged on William sighed. 'Well, there you
are,' he said evenly.

Very pale now, Stacie said: 'I'm sorry, William. I
can't talk about it and it isn't as simple as you seem to
think—there's nothing I can say. I'm not ... Nicholas
and I aren't ... oh, it's all too complicated, I can't
explain.'

'No explanation needed,' said William, putting down
what was left of the grapes.

'William, I am sorry . . .'

'Oh, I'll get over it, my heart's not broken or any of that stuff,' he told her, getting up. 'I'll miss you, but I hope you'll be happy, although I don't see you with a guy like that. I hope you know what you're doing, he isn't the type to stay faithful for long and I hate to think of you getting hurt, but be happy—look after yourself, and don't pull any more crazy stunts like this, stay out of line when the firing starts next time!' He kissed her lightly and was gone before she could think of anything to say, and it was probably better not to drag it out, so she sat and watched the door close with tears in her eyes.

She cried a lot lately; she tried to hide it from the hospital staff because she was furious with herself for such stupid weakness, but sometimes they noticed the tearstains. 'Oh, it's perfectly normal,' her bossy nurse told her complacently. 'It's all part of the healing process. You aren't yourself and you cry easily, anything will trigger off tears when you're ill.'

'How comforting,' Stacie said bitterly, and the nurse laughed.

'I can see you're getting better! It won't be long before we see the back of you.'

'Don't sound so eager,' said Stacie as the girl tucked the bedclothes tightly around her. 'When *will* I be allowed to go home?'

'Don't ask me, ask the doctor.'

'I will,' said Stacie, and when she next saw the doctor she asked him when she would be allowed to leave. He smiled at her condescendingly and told her she would be the first to know when he decided she was fit enough to go home.

'Of course, you won't be able to go back to work for a while. You won't have the use of your left arm until that shoulder has completely healed. Do you have a family to visit for a few weeks of convalescence?' The

Ward Sister moved slightly, giving an attention-attracting little cough, and the doctor looked round, raising one brow. Stacie watched him exchange a long look with the Sister and apparently read some silent message in her eyes. He looked thoughtfully back at Stacie and smiled. 'Of course, I'd forgotten,' he murmured. 'Well, we'll see—don't worry, we don't want our beds occupied for a second longer than we think is absolutely necessary. We'll push you out of here as soon as we can.'

Before they left London, Stacie's parents had suggested she stay with them when she got out of hospital, but she had been reluctant to accept the invitation. It was a long drive to Northumberland, at this time of year it would be freezing cold up there; and her mother wasn't as strong as she liked to believe, and Stacie didn't want to add to her work. She knew her mother would insist on waiting on her hand and foot and refuse to let her help in any way. When she gently tried to explain without hurting her mother's feelings Mrs Murray had looked upset, until Helen intervened.

'She must come to us, she'll need to have that dressing changed every day, and Roland's nurse can pop in and see to it without any trouble. Apart from that you never know what problems will show up after something like this—and Roland will be around to catch any symptoms before they get worse.' Helen had laughed at Stacie. 'Handy to have a doctor in the house!'

'Oh, well, I suppose that's true,' Mrs Murray had agreed reluctantly.

'When I'm fit I'll come up and see you,' Stacie promised in a placating voice. She would rather stay with her sister, Helen wouldn't fuss over her or try to confine her to bed half the time. Stacie could babysit and let Helen and Roland have some time together, she wouldn't feel such a burden if she was allowed to help with whatever tasks a one-armed person could perform. If she knew Helen, she would be learning how to peel potatoes with one hand in no time.

While Helen was in London, she had gone along to Stacie's flat and packed a case of clothes for her—mostly nightgowns to wear instead of the starched white hospital gowns that made Stacie feel like a convict, but the case had also held a skirt and sweater and a blouse and some silky underwear for the day when she was allowed to dress and leave the hospital. It was more than a week before the Ward Sister produced the case and smilingly told Stacie that she could go home.

'When? Tomorrow? I must ring my sister, she's going to drive up to fetch me,' Stacie explained. She had had no warning that she was about to be discharged.

'No need for that—a car has been ordered. It will take you wherever you want to go. It should be here in half an hour, so get dressed, Miss Murray.' The Ward Sister gave her a dry little smile that held curiosity.

'A car? Who . . .' Stacie bit the question off, flushing as she met the other woman's quizzical eyes. She didn't need to have the question answered; she knew Nicholas had provided the car, just as he had had her brought here and had paid all her bills. It was generous of him and she shouldn't resent it, because she knew he was doing it because she had saved his life, but Stacie prickled at the look she was getting from the Sister. She hadn't set eyes on Nicholas since the night she woke up to find him in her room, but he had been present in her head all that time, and she despised her own weakness.

'Do you need help with dressing?' the Sister asked, and Stacie shook her head.

'I can manage, thank you.' She had been out of bed and able to walk to the bathroom across the corridor for several days, but when the Sister had left and she began to get ready she found herself trembling, her legs weak underneath her. It was the excitement of going home, she told herself firmly. The sooner she was out of here the less she would owe Nicholas Kinsella; her bill must be astronomical.

She was going to insist on repaying him, but she would contact him formally, through a lawyer; she wasn't going to risk a personal contact. Staring angrily at her flushed face in the tiny mirror in the room, she pulled her sweater over her head with a vicious tug. Why couldn't she just forget him? What right did he have to order a car for her? She hadn't been consulted; if she had, she would have refused point-blank and made her own arrangements. Sometimes she felt afraid, she woke up in the night, trembling, feeling the tentacles of Nicholas's power closing around her. He had always got what he wanted; he didn't have the ability ordinary people learn so soon, to accept when he was beaten and give up. Nicholas had a sort of fierce tenacity; he had stayed away from her since that night they talked in here, but she hadn't felt that he had really gone. She was here because he wanted her here and she knew him well enough by now to be certain he meant to fight to keep her in his power. William had probably been quite right when he said it had been Nicholas who made sure he was denied admittance to her in the hospital. Stacie felt Nicholas looming behind her, like a black shadow, arranging and controlling her life even when she was unaware of it.

'How are you getting on?' The nurse had come into the room suddenly and Stacie jumped at the question. 'Hey, your nerves are bad!' the nurse exclaimed, staring at her. 'Anything I can do? Are you ready? Your car is here.'

'Thank you for everything you've done,' said Stacie, offering her hand and smiling.

The nurse carried her case along the corridor, with Stacie walking carefully and slowly behind her. She still

felt unsteady and the light seemed oddly brilliant
although it was a grey January day. She blinked at the
windows, amazed by the cold sunlight which suddenly
shone for a moment; everything looked so bright and
clear and sharp as though she had never seen the world
before.

She had to go to the Ward Sister's office to collect
her medicine, sign her discharge papers and have a final
lecture on being sensible and taking care of herself from
the Sister before she could escape into the cold daylight.
The nurse walked beside her, carrying her case in one
hand while with the other she steered Stacie as though
she might not be able to make it alone. As they emerged
Stacie saw the black limousine parked outside and
stopped, her eyes nervous and her limbs trembling,
backing like a panic-stricken horse that isn't quite sure
what is terrifying it.

'Don't stand around like that, you'll tire yourself—
get into the car,' the nurse scolded, handing her case to
the uniformed chauffeur. He walked round to stow it in
the boot and the nurse slid Stacie into the back of the
car with the deftness of someone used to moving inert
bodies about. She got no help from Stacie, who had
apparently lost the ability to move.

'Look after yourself, now,' the nurse told her
cheerfully before she closed the door. 'Don't do
anything I wouldn't do—and stay away from men with
guns in future!' She gave a coy look to the man beside
Stacie and winked.

The door slammed. Stacie sat rigidly staring straight
ahead. The chauffeur got behind the wheel; the
limousine smoothly moved away and the hospital
vanished from sight. The glass between chauffeur and
passengers was tightly closed.

'I want to go to my flat,' she managed to whisper at
last.

There was no reply, and that broke the spell holding

her. She looked round, her face angry. 'Did you hear what I said?'

It was a shock to her to look at him; the reality of Nicholas was even more powerful than the idea of him. Her senses went crazy and she swallowed, her throat dry.

'I've got to talk to you,' he said evenly, and although he spoke so quietly his grey eyes held an intensity of feeling that made her wince.

'We've got nothing to say,' Stacie whispered, but that wasn't true: there was too much to say, she wanted to tell him she loved him more than she could bear; he wasn't to look at her like that, he was torturing her, he was putting them both through a pain they didn't have to feel if only he would be rational and realise it wasn't possible for them to love each other.

'I've got a great deal to say,' Nicholas said with a steely note in his voice now. 'And I am going to say it, and nothing you can say will stop me this time.'

'It's pointless, you're just wasting your time!' She dragged her eyes away from the magnet of his body and stared out of the window. 'Where are you taking me?'

'First to my flat to talk and then I'll drive you to your sister's.'

'Just take me straight to Helen's—please, Nicholas! I can't go through this again, I've stood enough!'

'You've stood enough?' he broke out. 'What about me? Do you think I'm going to walk away and never see you again? Don't you know what that would do to me? Stop pretending you don't feel like this, too; you can't hide it from me any more than I could hide it from you. We both know what's happened. I didn't realise just how badly you'd hit me until I saw you lying in that street covered in blood.' His voice sank, rough and hoarse. 'I almost went berserk—I thought you were dead and I was out of my mind with shock. Having come that close to losing you I knew I couldn't go through that again.'

She had gone white, shrinking from the force in the husky words, and Nicholas moved closer, staring at her trembling mouth with a hunger she couldn't pretend she didn't recognise. It was the same fierce compulsion she had known on the first night they met; she had felt it at first sight, it had been between them from the beginning, as immediate and instinctive as the most basic animal drive, but it was deeper now, everything that had happened between them had intensified that first stark attraction.

'Don't, please, don't,' she pleaded, and felt him tense, struggling to regain control. He turned and looked out of the window, his hands clenching on his knees. The car slowed and turned into the drive of a large apartment block. It parked outside the main entrance and the chauffeur got out and walked round to open their door. Nicholas was already out of the car, he reached her door and gently helped her to climb out, while the chauffeur stared woodenly over their heads.

'We'll be leaving for Norfolk in an hour,' Nicholas told her as he turned towards the building.

The chauffeur watched them walk away. Stacie was trembling so hard she had to lean on Nicholas's support; inside her head she was trying to martial her arguments, think of a way of convincing him without admitting how deeply she was involved with him; Nicholas must never know that. He must not be certain she loved him or he would never let her go.

'I've got an apartment on the top floor,' he said as they went into the lift. The doors closed and Stacie leaned against the wall, a few feet away from him, her mind working chaotically.

'When are you going home?' she asked.

'Next week I'm off to Sydney for a few days and I have to be in Chicago the week after that.' He looked round at her grimly. 'That's why I have to talk to you today. I'd have waited until you were stronger, if I could, but there's no time.'

The lift stopped, they walked across the wide corridor on the top floor and Nicholas let them into an apartment opposite the lift. 'I've rented this place from a friend for a month,' he told her. 'Let me take your coat; the central heating is very good, the apartment's like a hothouse.' He carefully slid her jacket off and laid it over a chair in the square sitting-room. 'Sit down, Stacie, you look tired,' he said with concern, staring at her pale face.

'I am tired,' she said. 'Nicholas, don't put me through this, please . . .'

'You need a brandy,' he said, and walked over to a black oak cabinet. She watched despairingly as he produced a decanter and two glasses.

'It's too early,' she protested, but she was shaking so much she had to sit down. The furniture was ultra-contemporary; deeply upholstered in suede so soft it felt like white velvet as she ran a hand over it. Her body relaxed into the yielding warmth and she put her head back, sighing. The whole room was in black and white; there were modern paintings on the walls whose wild whorls of colour underlined the starkness of the domino principle everywhere else.

'I couldn't live in a room like this,' she said drily, and Nicholas smiled as he came back towards her with a brandy glass in each hand.

'Rather alarming, isn't it?' He sat down beside her, handing her one glass. 'Drink it,' he insisted. 'It's what you need.'

She sipped, making a face. 'I don't think my doctor would approve.'

Nicholas drank his brandy in two swallows and put the glass down. Stacie shrank back into the corner of the couch as he twisted towards her, an arm along the back of it.

'Marianne went back to Boston two days ago,' he said coolly, his grey eyes noting her rigidity without comment. 'We talked frankly before she left and we agreed we weren't suited. The marriage is off, and Marianne seems quite cheerful about it, so she needn't worry you any more.'

Stacie drank some more brandy. It helped her to say unsteadily: 'It makes no difference, it had nothing to do with Marianne.'

'You aren't in love with this reporter,' Nicholas said impatiently. 'Don't tell me you are!' Stacie finished her brandy before she answered him.

'I wasn't going to, William is nothing to do with it, either.'

He ran a hand through his black hair, raking it into disorder. 'Then what is it, for heaven's sake?'

Stacie looked into her empty glass and wished she had some more brandy; she needed the courage it seemed to give her. 'I'd hate it,' she muttered. 'Don't you see? I'd be out of place and all your friends would cold-shoulder me, your mother doesn't like me much, either, she certainly wouldn't be pleased. What would I do with myself all day when you were working or flying around the world? What sort of life would that be? I'd be miserable, and everyone would disapprove . . .'

'What has it got to do with anyone but us?' Nicholas exploded. 'Are you crazy? I'm not hearing this, I don't believe my ears.'

'Oh, don't be stupid, Nicholas . . .' she flared, glaring at him.

'Me stupid? What do you think you are?'

'I'm being rational,' Stacie said defiantly.

'Rational? That's a new name for it. It used to be called stupidity.'

She was flushed at the scathing note in his voice. 'You can't deny your mother doesn't like me, and wants me out of your life?'

'I've got news for you,' he said tersely. 'What my mother wants doesn't matter as much as what I want. I stopped asking her permission to do anything a long, long time ago. I don't let her pick my friends, and as sure as hell she isn't going to pick my wife for me.'

'She picked Marianne and you let her!'

'That was a mistake and I soon realised it. I wouldn't use that as an example if I were you.' His eyes challenged her and she looked away.

'Nicholas, I couldn't cope with the way you live,' Stacie sighed in a weary voice. 'I just could not cope.'

'You coped with that guy who tried to kill me the other day,' he said. 'You coped with Roughton—he's scared stiff of you. He'd rather quarrel with a wildcat than tangle with you again. I'd say you could cope with anything life threw at you.' He lowered his hand and she felt it stroke gently over her hair. 'You're quite something, Stacie; I've never met a girl like you, and if you think I'm going to let you kick me out of your life now you don't know me very well yet.'

He moved closer, she felt his thigh pressing against her own and shuddered. 'Don't,' she whispered as his hand closed round her waist.

'Don't what?' Nicholas asked, his lips on her throat.

'You're forgetting my shoulder,' she reminded him. 'I mustn't tear the stitches.' Her voice was barely audible, she found the warm slide of his mouth across her skin breathtaking.

'Don't struggle then,' he murmured complacently, and she put a hand on his chest to push him away, but it was like trying to push over a mountain. He just moved even closer and his lips crawled up her chin towards her mouth.

'This isn't going to solve anything,' she wailed.

'Wrong,' said Nicholas, and his mouth found hers and her arm weakly went round his neck as she melted under the kiss she had been needing for days. 'It will solve everything,' he whispered against her mouth.

When Stacie had stood in the street and realised that someone was going to kill him she had been filled with grief and terror and despair; she had run screaming his name, knowing at that instant just how fiercely she loved him. She didn't scream his name now; she kissed him back, craving his mouth with a need so intense that it was like dying, and she didn't want him to stop kissing her because when their mouths parted she would be cold and sick with need, and she would have to say goodbye to him.

Nicholas gently drew away a few moments later, and looked down at her flushed face. She opened her eyes with reluctance and couldn't stop herself from looking back at him with answering passion.

'I love you,' he said.

'You can't . . .'

'But I do,' he said with a wry patience like someone talking to a beloved idiot. 'And I think you love me. Why won't you admit it?'

'I can't love you,' she said, trying to move away, and he tethered her more firmly in his arm, his free hand brushing back the hair from her face.

'Are you scared, Stacie?'

She didn't answer, but her eyes spoke for her, as they had so many times before, when they wordlessly understood each other.

'I don't believe it,' he said, smiling. 'You? Scared? What of, for heaven's sake?'

'Getting hurt,' she whispered, hating to admit it, and as his face changed she talked hastily to bury that shameful admission under a mound of words. 'It wouldn't work—we don't really know each other, it's crazy to talk of being in love, what do you know about me? What do I know about you? We might quarrel all day long, we . . .'

He put a finger on her mouth and she stopped talking instantly; electrified by the touch of his flesh on her own.

'Stacie, do you love me?' he asked, and her eyes were fixed on the warm, hard curve of his mouth, remembering the feel of it and the necessity of having it touching her. The minute she saw him she had felt a need to touch him, to become part of him, it terrified and haunted her.

'That isn't fair,' she mumbled against his finger, and kissed his cool skin at the same time, while Nicholas watched her intently.

'You do, don't you? I love you and you love me. What could be more simple?'

'You don't understand!' she wailed.

'Explain it to me, then. Tell me why you're such a coward about love. Nobody gets a cast-iron guarantee for the future, Stacie. I could get shot tomorrow.'

She winced, white to her hairline and he looked at her tenderly.

'So could you, my love—do you think I wouldn't want to die, too? Whatever you're afraid of, we'll face it together; nothing's so terrible that it can't be faced.'

Stacie looked at him helplessly, torn between her love and her fear of love, and his head began to come closer, she couldn't take her eyes from his mouth, her lips were parting, waiting for it.

'Give me one good reason why you can't love me,' Nicholas said huskily. 'Just one, Stacie—but it had better be a good one.'

Stacie needed that kiss too much. She closed her eyes and lifted her mouth to take his before it even reached her. 'I'll think of one tomorrow,' she said.

Coming Next Month in Harlequin Presents!

735 THE GREAT ESCAPE Amanda Carpenter
Can an American heiress escape from her fortune? Not when she is pursued from Kentucky to Ohio by a private detective. But can she believe his claim that he has her best interests at heart?

736 ONCE A LOVER Claire Harrison
He is no longer her husband, her lover or her friend. But he has the crazy idea that he can miraculously alter the past and give them a future together—as husband and wife.

737 DAWN OF A NEW DAY Claudia Jameson
A young woman's vacation in the Bahamas seems like a dream come true until she finds herself having to share her seclusion with a man who thinks she —like most women—finds him irresistibly attractive.

738 WANTING Penny Jordan
An English model meets her match when she unwittingly challenges the master of the game to her favorite sport of enticement and denial. Winner takes all . . . and she forfeits her heart!

739 WORKING RELATIONSHIP Madeleine Ker
Her love affair with film almost ends in Tibet when a filmmaker works alongside her idol, a legendary director. He sets impossible standards for her as a professional and as a woman.

740 A LOST LOVE Carole Mortimer
Her new face and new identity don't protect a desperate woman when she comes face-to-face and heart-to-heart with the one man who must never know that she is still alive—her husband.

741 RUN SO FAR Peggy Nicholson
A volunteer crisis-center worker loses her objectivity when her heart goes out to a man who is as much on the run as is his runaway son. The man is on the run from love!

742 ROUGH AND READY Elizabeth Oldfield
The life of a cashier in a fast Soho casino is no life for the respectable young widow of a policeman—according to the club's Welsh bodyguard. But why would a man like him even care?

Harlequin Celebrates *Thirty-five Years of Excellence*

6 TOP HARLEQUIN AUTHORS—6 CLASSIC BOOKS!

Join us in celebrating as we reissue six Harlequin novels by some of the best authors in series-romance-publishing history. These books still capture the delight and magic of love as much today as they did when they were originally published by Harlequin. The fact that they transcend time attests to their excellence.

THE 1950s
Nurse/Doctor books—
"delightful books with happy endings."

THE 1960s
An era of "armchair travel" and exotic settings for Harlequin readers

THE 1970s
Harlequin becomes a household word and introduces Harlequin Presents— today, still the most popular series of contemporary romance fiction

THE 1980s
World-renowned authors continue to ensure Harlequin's excellence in romance series publishing

1. GENERAL DUTY NURSE
   by Lucy Agnes Hancock

2. HOSPITAL CORRIDORS
   by Mary Burchell

3. COURT OF THE VEILS
   by Violet Winspear

4. BAY OF NIGHTINGALES
   by Essie Summers

5. LEOPARD IN THE SNOW
   by Anne Mather

6. DAKOTA DREAMIN'
   by Janet Dailey

Available now wherever paperback books are sold or available through Harlequin Reader Service. Simply complete and mail the coupon below.

Harlequin Reader Service

In the U.S.
P.O. Box 52040
Phoenix, AZ 85072-2040

In Canada
P.O. Box 2800, Postal Station A,
5170 Yonge Street, Willowdale, Ontario M2N 5T5

CEL-1

Please send me the following editions of <u>Harlequin Celebrates 35-Years of Excellence</u>. I am enclosing my check or money order for $1.50 for each copy ordered, plus 75¢ to cover postage and handling.

1 ☐   2 ☐   3 ☐   4 ☐   5 ☐   6 ☐

Number of books checked _____ @ $1.50 each = $_____
N.Y. state and Ariz. residents add appropriate sales tax $_____
Postage and handling $ .75
I enclose _____   TOTAL $_____

(Please send check or money order. We cannot be responsible for cash sent through the mail.) Price subject to change without notice.

NAME _____
(Please Print)

ADDRESS _____ APT. NO. _____

CITY _____ STATE/PROV. _____ ZIP/POSTAL CODE _____

BARBARA DELINSKY
Fingerprints

Carly Quinn is a
woman with a past.
Born Robyn Hart, she
was forced to don a new
identity when her intensive
investigation of an arson-ring
resulted in a photographer's death
and threats against her life.

Ryan Cornell's entrance into her life
was a gradual one. The handsome
lawyer's interest was piqued, and then
captivated, by the mysterious Carly—a
woman of soaring passions and a
secret past.